GOLD

is for

GREED

GOLD IS FOR GREED

Want to know about Michael's new books?
Sign up for his new release newsletter at:
kowalkowal.com

Telling
Stories
Press

Other Books By Michael Kowal

YOUR FREE BOOK IS WAITING

It's 1930s Los Angeles and ex-Marine, and current PI, John Devin tackles his first case... to get back a very big diamond, for a pain in the neck friend.

But the diamond leads Devin on a chase through LA that eventually leads to Chinatown - and the leader of its underworld.

Sometimes people are brought together for a reason - and sometimes the reason... is to die.

★ ★ ★ ★ ★

"Grabs you from the beginning and doesn't let up."

Get Both!

INCLUDES - The Bonus Story: Bennie!
A batch of stolen money leads Devin straight to Bennie... one of my favorite characters in Red is for Blood.

Your free novel - Red is for Blood - is waiting for you,

along with the short story Benny, at:

kowalkowal.com/free-book

Get Them Now!

(And check out the end of this book for a sample of

Red is for Blood...)

Acknowledgments

First off I'd like to thank my amazing first readers, and master turnaround artists — Lee Ann and Mike — you were both heroes this time. Your perfect insights helped make this a much better book. Thank you.

A great big thanks to Bob@LAPoliceMuseum for taking the time to answer all my questions, plus all the extras that have helped make Devin and 1930s LA even richer.

To Allyson Longueira, for all of her publishing, design, marketing, and promotion knowledge that she freely shares, so many thanks. And to Colleen Kuehne and her copy editing skills, a thanks that's raised to the sky.

Kristine Kathryn Rusch, Dean Wesley Smith, and ML Buchman — I keep thanking them and I will continue to do so. Their skill as writers, storytellers, publishers, and business people is immense, but that is only eclipsed by their generosity as people and friends. I cannot thank each of you enough.

And finally, and most importantly — to my wife. The love, and support, and kindness that she continues to give me is the reason I am able to do what I do. Thank you, and I love you. Always.

To Sheldon McArthur
for his spirit, kindness, and most of all
for reminding me why I tell stories…

Chapter 1

I WOKE TO DROOL on my calendar.

The calendar on top of my desk. The one my face, and the drool, were plastered against.

I must have fallen asleep. A not too hard thing to do when you haven't slept in three days. Except, apparently, something happened last night as I worked.

It was day, and a crick in my neck let me know this wasn't going to be a good day.

"Mornin', sunshine."

Bella.

I cracked my eyes a bit, enough to see Bella standing in the open door to my office. She was sideways.

So I picked up my head.

Bad mistake.

The crick in my neck shot down to my lower back like a knife trying to find a home. It found it, and hurt like hell.

But at least Bella was now upright, the main reception area of John Devin Investigations behind her.

The sun shone in through the window to my right. It looked out onto 7th Street and from the sounds of it, life was in full swing. Even if I was having trouble joining it from the edge of my own desk.

Apparently, my bed for last night.

I'm not sure how much sleep I got last night, probably about an hour, but I'd gotten none for the previous two nights. So an hour over three days. Wonderful.

I was sure I was going to die.

But it was hard to leave the office when you were as busy as I was. I had solved a high-profile multiple murder case, and that seemed to have brought out the papers. And along with the stories, came the cases.

And I wasn't looking a gift horse in the mouth. Not in a depression. I would take all I could get. I had people depending on me.

Bella looked at my mouth, and a thin line of spit still hanging from it. "Now that's nice. I haven't seen something like that since I went to visit my sister last year. Except her son was five months old. And you're what?"

"About to fire your backside."

"Promises."

Bella always looked perfect — perfect lipstick, perfect makeup, perfect skirt, and perfect blouse. The lipstick was red this morning as it always was, the eye makeup subdued and slightly blue, her blouse white, and her skirt a deep navy blue that dropped down to her knees. She was a year younger than me, but she also carried around a lot of pain and hard life in her. So a lot of people read her as older. But they always saw her strong beauty. She was tall for a woman and big boned, in a very feminine way, with all the curves in all the right places. And she was like an older sister to me. A big pain-in-the-backside one.

"You want coffee?"

I gave her a look like that was about the craziest question in the history of questions. "Yeah."

Then she disappeared out the door. We had gotten a small hotplate and a coffeepot. Her idea. She said it would welcome potential clients as they came in the door.

I'm not sure how many detective agencies in LA offered coffee, but at least I had as much as I wanted. And didn't have to go to a diner to get it. Maybe Bella was pretty smart after all. Actually, she was smarter than me. I was just the lunk that went out to solve the cases. Mostly by ramming my head into it as many times as it took to get it done. It's what I learned in the Marines — brute force gets a lot done. Especially when it's a city like LA, where most of the time the cases wanted to knock you right back. Or sometimes try to kill you.

I looked at my desk and I had three piles of paper and files sitting on it. The one that I had almost drooled on, the Sanchez case, was a simple matter of finding one Mr. Arelio Sanchez. Who had apparently lost himself on the way back from a trip to the market for a pack of cigarettes.

I had half a mind that Mr. Sanchez wasn't ever coming back, but with Mrs. Sanchez footing the bill for the investigation, I owed it to her to find out for sure.

On the one hand, I had found out that he owed a few gambling debts around town. But on the other, he had also been making time with a certain prostitute down on Central Avenue by the name of Trixie. Trixie had also disappeared.

Convenient.

I was also working to find a stolen bracelet and on a blackmail case. Plus five others.

All in all, the high-profile murder investigation had gotten me all of this. But they paid the bills, kept Bella paid, kept me with a roof over my head, and kept a young kid named Charlie off the streets and working here. At least with whatever Bella found for him to do.

A lot of mouths to feed.

And not a family to my name.

Life was okay. If I could just get some sleep. But who else

was going to get all this done?

"You really ought to let me help with some of that." Bella had come back into my office and laid a steaming cup on my desk calendar. Right over the darkened drool mark. At least she covered it. Maybe taking care of me in yet another way.

I checked the clock on the wall and it was 7:45 a.m. and the office hadn't even opened yet.

But that didn't stop the outer office door from pushing open tentatively.

In walked a fragile looking old woman.

She was worn and wrinkled, looking like the entire weight of the world was on her. She looked past Bella and straight to me.

"Mr. Devin?"

Chapter 2

BELLA WALKED OUT INTO the reception area and closed my door behind her.

I heard low murmurs from the other side of the door, a bit about "Sorry I came in so early," and other things whispered softly.

There was back and forth out there between Bella and the woman.

I kept focusing on the Sanchez case, the Crouse case, and the Hanson case, and my mind couldn't decide which one it wanted to abuse itself with. I was tired of them all.

I was thankful for the cases, for the business, but it was tough.

I hadn't gotten a good night's sleep in five days, and no sleep in the past three. Except for the drool nap I seemed to have taken last night. Judging from the clock, for maybe about an hour. But you don't turn down business just because you want to get a decent night's sleep on your own fold-away Murphy bed.

I'd forgotten what it even felt like.

A small tap sounded at the frosted glass of my door, and Bella slipped into my office and closed the door behind her. I looked up. "Bad check, or someone else lose a husband?"

Bella's face turned up a bit and I wasn't sure if it was because the woman had something bad, or she didn't want to bother me with it.

I sat back in my chair. "Go ahead, what is it?"

"Remember that Liliana McGann case a year ago?"

I thought back for a split second, then it hit me. Large. "Yeah." Liliana McGann had been the biggest starlet in Hollywood. Up until she got herself murdered a year ago. She had been out with friends, then came back late to her semi-famous restaurant. And was killed. "Fiancé did it, right?"

Bella flicked her head toward what was beyond the frosted glass door. "That's the fiancé's mother."

I couldn't figure out what she would be doing here. If the papers were right, and at least some of the time they were, her son was going to be hanged... tomorrow at midnight. Hmm... "What does she want?"

"Well..." Bella seemed like she couldn't believe it herself, "she wants you to clear her son."

I laughed. I hadn't laughed in at least five months. And that was a first.

I didn't laugh because it was funny, I laughed because it was... today. Pretty much a day and a half until he was hanged. Seemed a little late for miracles. "You're kidding, right?"

"She says she's been to every other agency in town."

"And they all gave her the answer I would give her. Can't you just—"

The door cracked open and the small woman, carrying a small black book and a file full of papers, walked in with no small determination in her soft blue eyes.

Eyes lit like a person who would stop at nothing to get what she... not wanted, that was too crass, but needed. And apparently, she wanted to help her son. "Mr. Devin?"

Bella turned to help the old woman out but I stopped her. "It's okay, Bella." It was my responsibility to break the woman's heart, not Bella's. My name was on the door. "I'm John Devin."

I got up from behind the desk and kept the coffee cup over the drool mark on the calendar. No need to look stupid as I broke the old woman's heart.

But I wasn't sure who was going to do the breaking.

The woman was tired and looked it. Maybe like me. And she didn't pay any attention to the seven safes that lined the walls of my office.

She wore no hat and her hair was pulled back severely, like on the farm. Keep things out of the way when you worked.

She was thin and gaunt. Her eyes were sunk in, her mouth, too, and the skin clung tight to her cheekbones. Like it was afraid to let go.

"Mrs…?"

"White."

"Mrs. White."

Her voice was soft, but it had something back of it.

She looked out of place in Los Angeles. Her dress was worn thin but clean. The small yellow daisies on her faded blue dress were faded at the collar, and faded even more at the edge of her sleeve as she held out her old and withered hand for me to shake.

I took it. It was warm. Very warm to almost hot.

But her grip was firm and I recognized her from the callouses on the inside of her hand. A person who did work. Hard work. Most likely a farm. "Please, have a seat."

She nodded as I directed her to one of the hard oak chairs I have in front of my desk. I keep them without a cushion to keep people from staying too long. But as she sat, I felt bad about that.

"So," I began as I got back into my own chair behind the desk, "what can I do for you?"

She sat there on the other side from me, a small, dried piece of grass that looked like it was at the end of its life.

She set the black book and file up on top of my desk. I left the two of them there. I wasn't about to touch them. I only let her in to let her down soft.

She sat straight on the edge of the seat and looked at me sharp, her eyes looking an even lighter blue as they somehow took on more life. "I know what you're going to say. I've been told it by all of them."

"Who?"

She smiled, not baring the inside of her mouth. A practiced smile. One to not reveal what may or may not be left inside her mouth. But a smile it most definitely was. "Every other detective in Los Angeles." Then her smile went flat.

"And your son is…?"

"I can hear." She nodded toward my office door. "Your secretary already told you that."

I had badly underestimated a certain piece of dried grass sitting in front of me.

"And she's nice."

I laughed a little. "And I'm not?"

Mrs. White glared at me from inside those sunken sockets. "That just depends."

I couldn't quite make out who was sitting in front of me. A broken down woman, or some kind of predator that LA hasn't seen in its entire life. A home-spun backside kicker. I liked her right away.

She reminded me of a grandmother I'd never had — and would have wanted. "Do you know the case?"

This really was moving a little faster than I wanted. And it must have been because I hadn't slept last night… or because my desk had flattened the inside of my head… but this little meeting was quickly getting away from me. I hoped my own bleary eyes didn't give away how sleepy I was.

"You look like crap."

So much for that. "Look, Mrs. White, if getting down to brass tacks is what you like, then I know that your son is due to be executed… tomorrow?"

"Yes. Midnight."

"So I don't know how I could possibly help you with anything."

"They railroaded him."

"Who?"

"Everybody."

"Everybody covers a lot of people."

"Well there were a lot of people who did it."

"And do you have proof?"

My guess was she didn't. Otherwise she would have brought it to the police already. Or at least if not the police, if there were some of them doing the railroading — a not uncommon thing in LA — then her lawyer should have gone to the judge.

She pointed at the book and the file sitting between us. "It's in there. All of it."

I sighed. I was tired. And I just wanted to go to bed.

And I did *not* want to touch that pile of papers. "Mrs. White, I already have too many cases. I slept on the desk last night—"

"You look like it."

"And while I'm sure your son is innocent—"

"His name is Miles."

"Miles, fine, all right. While I'm sure Miles is innocent—"

"You don't believe it for a minute."

I was losing my patience. "No, I don't. Not for one minute."

"Well, I do. He is innocent, Mr. Devin. No matter what you, or any other detective — or any lawyer or judge or lying newspaper here in this God-forsaken city — says."

Her eyes started to glisten. And I didn't like that.

"I have been to every detective in this city and, unfortunately, Mr. Devin, you are the last one left. The only one left. You will take this case and look into it or… or…"

Then the small, frail, piece of iron-centered grass started to break. Right in front of me.

It was first a small sniff, then one tear dropped. A fat and very full one. Then one more tear fell. Then another, and then the rest fell, all of them. All of them in a hot shower that rolled down her wrinkled and tired face.

All of the tears that I'm guessing she had been holding onto for… maybe longer than her entire life.

And she never let her gaze leave my eyes.

Her face stood rock still. Her head never once daring to hang itself in shame. The woman wept right there in front of me. Quiet. And as unmoving as the dirt is hard.

She just sat there and bared her soul to me.

Damn her.

Not since I was in the trenches back in the war, in France in 1918, had I ever felt this tired. There, it was for survival but here, in my office, I suppose it was for survival in another way.

In a time of general hopelessness, in the Depression, when nobody could get a job and two people's jobs — and my own — depended on me to keep this place open, I was just tired. And there was no way, no way at all, that I could in any good mind even think to look at this case.

Because everything else would fall.

Because there was only me. Only me.

I had to keep this place afloat. And I couldn't take this case no matter what.

So I watched, through the crazy half-asleep fog that clouded my mind, as I reached my hands out to the black book and the file folder underneath it, and pulled them back to me. Across the frayed calendar with countless marks and circles, the cryptic notes to Bella and myself laid across it. The notes of things I still needed to do, and all the days that had slid by me as I tried to keep a detective agency afloat.

By myself.

And suddenly the black book and the file were right in front of me.

It was just one look.

That's all I would do.

And after all, what harm could that do?

As it turned out, only everything.

Chapter 3

I LET MRS. WHITE out the main door and turned around to Bella sitting at her desk.

She put her hand on the black and chromium pen set that sat on the desk in front of her. Then she pushed it a little to the right. It was a sign — that things were rough and stormy.

In an office like this, there are a lot times that you can't exactly say what you want to say. Like if a client is sitting there in the office, or you're thinking maybe someone is out in the hallway listening in. So Bella and I came up with a few ways we could communicate. She moves her pen set to the left a little, things are cold and gloomy. Like maybe a client is sitting in there waiting to talk with me, she'll give me the sign. To know which way the wind is blowing.

But as I looked around the office, there were no clients. Just her and me.

Her. Rough and stormy.

Things weren't looking too good for me.

"Well..." Bella's brown eyes were razor sharp behind the tasteful makeup around it, her red lips thin and pulled in. Like she wanted to bite my head off.

"Before you get started on me, Bella, something is telling me she's telling the truth."

"Well I don't care if all of Los Angeles says she's telling the truth — I care about what you're already supposed to be doing."

It's funny how Bella always manages to sound like an older sister, even though she's a year younger than me. But I always take it. It's always the only option. Like a storm, you needed to just sit there and let it blow itself out.

"Who's going to finish all the other cases?"

See, that's where the logic part of her argument always seemed to come in. Right when I was digging in my heels. And the trouble was, her logic was always pretty sound. Like this time.

I hated that about her. She was smart, and knew how to use it.

And she kept going. "Take the Hanson case alone. That's going to take you another day and a half."

I thought it would take more like half a day tops.

"And if you're thinking it will take you half a day — tops — you my friend, are dreaming."

I forgot that part.

She also read minds.

And I hated that about her, too. "Look, Bella, I already have the list of all his old addresses. It's not going to take—"

"Well I looked at the addresses. Two are in Pasadena, one in Long Beach, and another one in Glendale for good measure."

"I'll do the Glendale ones right after Pasadena."

"I've already mapped it out myself, and it will take you a day and a half. And you promised Mrs. Hanson you would have her your report tomorrow."

"Tell her it'll be Friday."

"I did — last week, sunshine." Bella crossed her arms in front of her and leaned back in her chair. "And I'm not going to put her off again. Mostly because she is not a nice woman. Do you know how many people I—"

"Bella, the more I stand here, the longer it's going to take me to get to the prison."

"Okay! Fine. Then if you want to be stupid, what can I do?"

She sat there defiantly, her arms still crossed in front of her, her cheeks now looking a little red. That only happened when she was really mad.

And that was something you never wanted to make Bella.

Because then she started throwing things. Okay, maybe not throwing things, but she did look mad enough to throw me. Then the door opened behind me and Charlie walked in.

Young Charlie. Six foot like me and only fifteen. He had the heart of a teddy bear and the resilience of a mountain.

Charlie froze there in the door, looking at me, then at Bella. Then Bella pushed her pen set even more to the right. Charlie saw that, and walked right back out the door.

Traitor.

I turned back to Bella. I owned this office, damn it.

Except she commanded it. I know there is something wrong about that, but I never exactly got around to fixing it. Mostly because it worked. I left her to run things inside, while I took care of everything outside.

And besides, this was my agency. And I was the one responsible for it.

There was no one else to rely on for that. To get everything done out there, where everyone seemed to want to kill you. Especially these days.

I'd learned that a long time ago.

Never rely on anyone else. If you were responsible for it all.

Bella's face finally softened. "Let me run something down for you. Anything. Charlie can answer the phone if I need to go out. You can't do it all by yourself, John."

But I knew it different — it *was* my responsibility. "No." And that was that.

I guess I really was mad. Because I slammed the door a little too hard when I left.

The sound of the slam rang down the hallway.

Reminding me that no one does my work.

Ever.

It's the way it had always been. It's the way it would always remain.

Me.

Chapter 4

I GOT TO MECKLENBURG Prison an hour later. A nearly new monstrosity of concrete, dropped right at the beginning of the high-desert, and surrounded on all sides with a twenty-foot-tall gleaming silver fence.

The fence didn't bother me so much, but the barbed wire sitting on top of it did. It sat bright like the fence in the hot desert sun, reminding me of all the barbed wire I'd crawled over in the war. Over there the barbed wire was something I wanted to get into, to kill the Germans on the other side. Here, I wasn't too excited about going inside.

Except I'd promised a mother that I would.

A forty-foot solid concrete wall sat fifty yards inside the wire fence, and I could just make out the top of the prison inside that.

Because it was in the desert, the people who built the Meck realized, way too late, that it would end up baking every prisoner inside in the head. And the guards, too. So everybody was half angry, and half nuts, all the time. At least that's the way the newspapers talked about it.

I pulled up near the front gate of the wire fence where they had a small bit of parking available. Not too many people came up here to the threshold of the desert, so it was plenty open and a I took a spot next to an old black Ford truck.

I checked in with the guard at a small door in the fence and he waved me toward the massive concrete wall inside.

There were no windows in the wall and it looked like a castle. No way in, except the small hard metal door a ways in front of me.

I saw five guards walking the top of the wall in the baking sun, all of them looking back inside the wall. Each of them held a black Thompson submachine gun, their barrels pointed toward what was inside. I thought of castle guards of old, looking outward to protect from whatever was outside the walls. Here, they looked back inside to protect the rest of us on the outside. An odd turn.

From the outside, the massive, smooth-sided concrete wall had no way in or out except for the single door that lay in front of me. The wall was big, like the side of the troop ship I had shipped out to Europe on. I wondered how many prisoners they had here.

It didn't matter, more would always be coming.

They always did.

I checked in at the metal door in the wall and they even let me in there.

They would let anyone in.

Built five years ago, the Meck was meant to ease the load at San Quentin and Alcatraz to the north. See, LA nearly doubled our population, so now we got our very own prison to house all our very bad boys.

San Quentin was supposed to be the toughest in the system, but the Meck was harder. I suppose it went along with old Joseph Mecklenburg, who the prison was named after.

A dry, law and order sort, he was LA's chief of police twenty years ago and got himself shot dead in front of a line of police officers holding off a labor demonstration. Then they built this prison and named it after him.

I wondered what he would think about it.

After I knocked, the metal door opened and I was let into a

small wooden room with a counter and three guards. It smelled like three guards, and there wasn't much light in the place. Except for the single bulb trapped in its own cage in the middle of the ceiling. Apparently they were even concerned about the bulbs making a desperate escape.

I told them my business, that I wanted to meet Miles and that I was a PI. That didn't cut much with them, but when I mentioned the mother, they softened a bit. Apparently they liked her.

They hadn't expected any visitors. Miles had already said good-bye to his mother the day before, and told her he didn't want to see her again. I didn't want to think what that visit must have been like for her. But it's why she came to me.

With a few more calls, the guards got approval and found out where Miles was. Still eating breakfast. A day and a half from getting hanged by the neck probably made them a little more lenient. So they let me inside the Meck, and I headed off to find Miles, led by an escort.

Chapter 5

MILES WAS IN THE mess hall.

It was a large room with plain concrete walls, no windows, a concrete floor, and row upon row of dark, wooden mess tables bolted to the floor that stretched at least a hundred feet back into the cavernous room.

The tables were split into two sections, left and right, a large center aisle reaching to the back wall.

From the heavy smells that still hung in the air, breakfast must have consisted of burnt oatmeal and double-burnt coffee. It tore at my nose and hurt, but it brought back memories of being in the Marines. It was exactly the type of meal we would get, when we got any at all. A lot of memories came back. Some worse than others.

If I was counting, there had to be at least twenty rows of tables reaching back, and each table was thirty feet long. A lot of guys could be fed here, but at the moment there was only one, sitting in the back row on the left, with three guards standing behind him.

The guard in back of me tapped me on the shoulder, I looked back and nodded, then I made my way down the center aisle.

It all seemed a little lax for a prison known as the worst in California. The baby prison, only seven years old, but as hard and harsh as they could come.

As I approached, one of the three guards behind Miles, the shortest one, came up to meet me. "Hold it right there."

I did.

The guard got behind me and patted me down. The fifth time I'd been patted down this morning.

The guard finished with me, nodded, then motioned me forward.

Miles watched me walk up as he ate a piece of bacon. He was a young thing, maybe only twenty-two. His skin was smooth like nobody had a right to have, except actors in the pictures. But I didn't remember him ever being an actor. At least the papers didn't go on about it at the time, and that would have been something they would have.

He and Liliana had met in a restaurant, as the story went. He had been serving. He was a waiter.

"Who are you?" He spoke funny. Like someone trying to be from out east. He looked at me like he didn't care, although there probably wasn't much he cared about right now. The three fingers he held his piece of bacon in shined with grease.

He was probably five-six if he was standing, and probably weighed only a hundred and thirty. And looked like picking up that piece of bacon was putting a strain on him. As in he was lazy.

"John Devin. I'm a PI and your mother asked me to look into your case."

Miles rolled his eyes like a five year old. "I cannot imagine what my mother would have brought you in for."

"I think because she doesn't want to see you dead."

"Well…" Miles set down the bacon and picked up a small white mug of coffee and sipped at it, "then she's the only one." He looked off in the distance behind me, as if he were looking at a yacht race or something, then took another sip of coffee and set down the mug. The handle was now greasy, too.

Even though I came up here neutral, and in a way wanted to believe his mother, I was fast moving over to the camp that figured he was guilty. He had no will to live.

That was it — the accent he was trying for was Boston. But he was nowhere near it. It just came off as some kind of painted-on whitewash, trying to cover up a Florida pretty-boy hick come to the big city. He looked good, and that was about it. He was probably waiting for the pictures to find him, so when the biggest starlet in them found him instead, he went along for the ride.

"What do you have against your mother? She seems like a pretty nice woman to me. Especially since you don't have anyone else on your side."

Miles grimaced, his perfectly sharp upper-lip crinkling. He looked like a spoiled five year old with the body of a small man. "Mr... Devin is it? I left Florida when I was fifteen exactly to get out of that life. You couldn't blame me. Have you ever been to Florida?"

"No, I haven't."

"Well then, except for Miami, a little backwoods for me even, it is a glorified, humid, alligator and mosquito breeding farm. Pure and simple. It's the only thing they raise..."

His fake Boston accent was fading, and a hint of a Florida panhandle drawl started to seep in.

He took up his non-greasy hand and ran it through his hair in the manner of a young debutant by a pool. Then he wet his lips, too. What a show. "I left that woman because she refused to leave that man."

"What man?"

"My stepfather."

"So you left her there alone."

"She could have left."

This was getting uncomfortably close to a bad area for me. I decided to change tack. "Tell me about the lighter."

The lighter was an odd thing, but a pretty central thing, mentioned in Mrs. White's file and in her notes in the black book.

A small, bitter smile crossed Miles' face. "The one I had never seen my entire life?"

"That's the one."

Miles looked directly at me. "I never saw it my entire life." Then he smiled even more and put the last piece of bacon into the middle of it. The bacon disappeared. And the smile.

Bitterness didn't make him any more likable. Honestly, I wanted to smack him in the face. Instead, I chose honesty. "Look, I'm here because your mother asked me to talk to you, to take the case."

Miles got a bored look on his face. "Tell her to leave me alone."

"Look," I stuck both hands into my pockets so I wouldn't wrap them around his little neck, "your mother actually cares about you. Although from the looks of you, I can't see why she would. And honestly, if these guards weren't around, I'd like to give you the smacking around you deserve."

The big guard right in back of him shrugged. "Fine by us."

For a split second, I wanted to. Would have. But I thought of his mother. I came here to save him. For her.

The woman seemed like she'd gone through a life of loss, and if there was one more thing I could stop her from losing, I would. And in spite of him, I wasn't going to let her down.

Miles must have come to his senses because he actually wiped his greasy fingers off on his pant leg and looked at me. "Honestly, I never saw it before."

"Your mother said you don't even smoke."

"Never have."

I didn't either. Maybe he and I were the only two on the planet. At least I had something to relate to him on. My guess was it was going to be the only thing. "I assume you told the police."

"Yes. And my attorney. They didn't want to listen to me."

"Why?"

"That baffled me." Miles dropped his elbows to the table and, in a very improper way, sat there with his head resting in his hands like some starlet's pose for a glamor shot.

I wasn't sure where he got this stuff from. "Do you have any idea why?"

If the cops didn't chase down that part of the story, there was something else going on here. Like they didn't want to look at the details of the case too closely.

Miles looked at me and something seemed to leave him. Maybe it was his mask. He pushed the tray away a couple of inches and rested his arms on the table.

For the first time, he looked like he was actually there with me. "I gave up." And the southern accent that he had been trying to hide since I had been there, started to sneak out. Little, by little. "I realized soon that a... waiter from Florida, no matter how much he thought that the system was fair, was never going to get a fair shake. It was like I was a pawn. Do you read Shakespeare, Mr. Devin?"

The question surprised me. "No." I had, somewhere. I think my first year of high school. But it wasn't something that I ever thought about after that.

"Pity... he wrote some of the best characters in existence. Tragic, most of them really. Except for the comedies. Well, I loved Shakespeare and I always had a thought in my mind that I was like a character out of Shakespeare. With the whole world lined up against me."

Seemed like the kid loved drama.

"And soon, in the beginning of the trial, I began to see that this is what my life was. It was playing out exactly like that. It's like *The Tempest*. It was both comedy and tragedy, but I always thought it needed more of the tragedy to balance it out."

I didn't know what the hell he was talking about.

"And it was like that with my life. And in the middle of the trial, I began to see my life as a comedy that was really a tragedy."

I looked up at the big guard in back of Miles. He just shrugged, then went back to looking at the ceiling.

"Okay," I had to break up this little pity party, "What I need to know is, why did the cops — and your lawyer — not listen to you?"

Miles looked at me straight. "I don't know why."

"Come on, you had to have thought about it a little. They had you up for murder."

Miles just shrugged his shoulders.

He had completely given up. He really did see himself as some kind of tragedy. I hate people who give up. It's not something I ever do. "Okay, so let's take the cops out of this, and your lawyer. If you didn't do it, then who did?"

Miles sighed. "I've explained this to all the other detectives."

"Then why don't you tell me!" I really was about to smack him around.

Miles must have gotten the message. He straightened up a bit, at least a bit. It was an entire effort for him. "Who wouldn't want to? Liliana's business partners at the restaurant were constantly haranguing her to be there, but she was tired of it."

"Who are they?"

"Daisy and James."

"Business partners?"

Miles let out a small laugh. "Well, yes, but there was more. Daisy and James were married, even when Liliana slept with James."

Okay, that was interesting. "Is Daisy the jealous type?"

"Only of her own money. She could care less about James. She was more mad at Liliana for not showing up at the restaurant more, you know, to keep the people coming in. She used to be a hooker and had her life savings in the place. And she was not about to let Liliana ruin that."

"But she was okay to have Liliana ruin her marriage."

"She didn't ruin it. I think the only reason Daisy was with James was because he was a director. *Was* being the operative word, and she thought between him and Liliana, they would all bring in the great unwashed masses. And Daisy knew a good thing when she laid it." Miles smiled. "Oh, did I just say that?"

"You did."

Miles' smile got even bigger.

"You think Daisy could have killed her? Liliana?"

"Absolutely. A whore and her money are not easily parted."

The kid was definitely not Shakespeare. "Anyone else up for it?"

"Well, let's see — Dante Manzione ran a gambling operation on the third floor of the restaurant, Daisy and James were going after her every time she came in the place, and Louis Gold was mad at her because she wanted a new contract where he'd actually have to give her some real money. The kind of money she deserved. And she told each of them off that night."

Now I was remembering some of the particulars of the trial. Liliana had gone off half-cocked on a lot of people that night. A wonder what a party, a little booze, and a bad temper can do for you. But there was one other person he forgot to mention. "She told you off, too, from what I remember."

The smile on Miles' face dropped off a little, but then seemed to slide in just a bit, as if he were remembering. "Yes, she did." The memory must have played for a while, because he went quiet and stared off in back of me somewhere. As if reliving that night again.

Maybe he relived it a lot in here. Seemed like in prison, that was all you could do. As you waited for the knot to be tied onto you.

"She was tired of everyone that night. It started with me. Liliana came into the apartment above the restaurant, fresh from being battered by the wonder couple downstairs. She told them she wanted out. They told her she couldn't, that they didn't have the money to buy her out. So Liliana said that was okay, she would just take the kitchen equipment, all of it, in payment."

"She would sell it?"

Miles laughed. "Oh no, you didn't know Liliana. She would just drop it into the ocean. She was vengeful that way. She didn't care about the money. Did I tell you she wanted to be a teacher?"

"No."

"She did. That's all she ever wanted. When we used to lie awake in bed at night, she'd tell me what her childhood was like. How she loved her father and then, when he died, everything changed. She wanted to be a teacher, always had. But her mother entered her in a couple of Vaudeville competitions, and Liliana won. The mother saw a horse and rode it. All the way to Hollywood."

I only ever saw the funny Liliana. In the pictures.

"So Liliana was angry a lot of the time. After she came up to the apartment, she told me to get out, that she was moving back east. And she really was going to be a teacher. Then she told me she was breaking the contract with Louis, and going to kick Dante out of the third floor. Because she never really wanted him up there. It was all an idea that Daisy and James wanted. And Dante, too, truth be told. He knew having her around would only increase what he got at the tables."

"So instead you got drunk."

Miles looked back into that area behind me. "Yes."

"Do you even remember what happened?"

"I got drunk."

"After that."

Miles thought about it, like he'd probably thought about it every day since then. He told me like he was reading off a report. "I woke up to two cops breathing over me."

"And you didn't remember anything in between?"

Miles picked up another piece of bacon. He looked at it, not like he was hungry, but like he was just looking for something to do. "Mr. Devin—"

"Just Devin."

"All right then, Devin…" Miles looked around the cavernous mess hall, empty except for him, me, and four guards. Empty. His hand shook just the slightest bit as he held the bacon. "I feel that I am tired of lies." He still looked at me. "I… liked her. She was… famous."

I wasn't sure where this was going.

"When she first walked into the restaurant where I worked, I couldn't quite believe it. Liliana McGann, in my restaurant. She wore a silk dress the color of cream, with lace falling down from the neck and running down to the bottom. Her shoulders were bare, and her shoes were pure white. Small, like ballet slippers, I think. She saw me from across the room and immediately headed toward me. The gentleman she was with, I think an actor, a small actor, followed behind her. They fought as she walked up to a table near me and said she'd like to sit there. The gentleman went to take her chair but she insisted that I seat her."

I still wasn't sure what this even meant.

Miles continued. "She treated him poorly, like a dog, really. Paying attention to only me. A waiter. He got angry and eventually walked off in a huff, trying to save his pride." Miles looked back off into that middle distance and went silent for a while. Then he came back. "And that is when she collected me." Then Miles looked at me. "She liked to control things. She wanted him all to herself, until she didn't. Then she wanted me. Me."

Miles laughed, and there was a lot more to that statement… there was pride, and pain in what he said.

"I wanted the money, is that wrong?"

"Not exactly. A lot of people make a good living off it."

"But I did want more."

I looked around the mess hall. The Meck was certainly a lot more. Just not more of the things the kid had wanted. "Looks like you got it." I was about ready to leave, but I thought of one more thing. "If you had it to do over again, would you have?"

Miles sat there, the three guards in back of him, his fingers still glistening with bacon fat. "What, lived with her?"

"Yeah."

Miles looked at me, then down at his filthy fingers. His eyes didn't come back to mine, but he opened his mouth. And he spoke. Soft. "I did love her."

I waited for him to say anything else but he didn't. He kept his head bowed, maybe to a lot of regret.

I didn't know if he was telling the truth or not, but I did know one thing: if I wanted to save his backside for his mother, I couldn't be waiting around for any more answers from him.

I got out of there.

The smell of the place was getting to me.

And I had no clue what I was going to do next.

Chapter 6

I FIGURED THE NEXT step was to talk to the cops who handled the case. That lighter bothered me.

It's nice knowing cops. Well, a cop. Detective Cardon was someone who at least didn't want to arrest me every time he saw me. As a matter of fact, we'd even broken whiskey together.

I stopped off to talk with him, told him what I was up to, and while he rolled his eyes when I told him, he was at least a square enough guy to take me in to see the detectives. And it would end there. He promised.

He wasn't too well liked in the detective room, mostly I think because he was a square shooter. He'd always treated me square at least, and from what I could tell of him, he treated all of life that way.

He was a good guy, and he brought me into the detective room.

Not a large place, it was filled with dark oak desks, all of them at least thirty years old. They were dinged and gouged and shoved face to face in three rows, running up the middle and along the two sides. And that was the only organization the place had.

Each desk was piled and scattered with papers and files, most of the piles looking like they would topple at the slightest LA aftershock, let alone earthquake.

Three large floor fans pushed the stifling air of the room around, the cigar and cigarette smoke hanging thick and choking in the air.

All the detectives had their jackets off. White shirts and striped ones, solid colors and even a couple patterns, all of them had their ties loosened while most of their eyes were tight on me, even if they weren't facing me. They were an observant bunch.

Cardon led me to the back pair of desks along the right wall.

Two guys were behind the farthest desk, and I knew them. One, the shorter one, sat on the corner of the desk while the other, about the shape of a boulder, stood leaning into the corner, laughing at some joke the shorter one must have told.

They were by themselves and nobody else seemed to be interested in them.

Both were bald, the shorter one turning around and looking right at me. They looked like a matched set. Both had round faces, and both had their clean domes. Completely clean. I wasn't sure if they shaved them together or if they were sons of the same bald father.

Cardon pulled me up next to the desk. "Boys, this is Devin."

They looked at me like I was a dung-infested apple pie.

The shorter one, I liked to call Tweedle-Dee, stood up off the corner of the desk and tried to look dangerous. The other one, Tweedle-definitely-Dumb, looked at me without changing too much of his expression. Which meant that his mouth was still open. Like it was waiting for a fly to come home.

I put on my best Sunday-go-to-meetin' smile. "Boys." I even threw in a nod, because I was generous that way.

Cardon looked at Dee, "This is Price," then he looked at Dumb, "And this is Black."

I liked Tweedle-Dee and -Dumb better.

Cardon continued, "Devin's looking into the McGann murder."

Dee and Dumb looked at each other, and unless I was mistaken, a hard look passed between them that flashed past almost as quick as it had come. Then they lined up almost side-by-side. At least they tried to, on account of they were trapped between the desk and the wall.

They looked like a couple of kids caught at something. A couple of definitely mean kids.

"That was a long time ago." Dee's voice was higher than I'd expect from a rounded baldy. Like the sound a small bird would make if you crushed it.

"Yeah, a long time ago." Dumb's voice was deeper... like pretty much what you'd expect a boulder to sound like.

All in all, this sideshow was turning out more comical than what I'd imagined. "A year, as a matter of fact." I thought I'd throw that in just to refresh their memories.

Dee's voice was flat. "The guy's getting hanged tomorrow."

Okay, so Dee didn't so much need reminding. Interesting. After a year and who knows how many cases, he remembered this one. Of course, the newspapers had had it splashed all over the front pages for the past week.

The good old papers. Let's relive the murder of a starlet and sell a few papers in the process.

Cardon nodded at all of us. "I have things to do. Devin, you can get yourself out of here, right?"

I was touched by the gesture. "You afraid I'm going to get lost?"

"More afraid you won't. Just make it quick, then get lost." The smirk on his face let me know he was at least a little kidding. What a card.

Cardon left, and I was left with Dee and Dumb. They both looked at me like they were left with that pie — with the extras.

"The guy's about to die in..." Dee looked up at the huge white wall clock over the exit to the room—

"Tomorrow." Dumb helped him out.

"Yeah, tomorrow." Then Dee's face got even more nasty, his lips turning a brighter shade of red against the pasty white of his skin. "We got nothing to say to you."

"Yeah, nothing."

I kept wondering if these guys were muscle to some mobster, or if they really were detectives. I know there wasn't a huge bar to get into the LAPD — at least from what I could tell by the specimens I saw in front of me. But at least Cardon had sense and used it all the time.

My mother always said to treat idiots nicely. She didn't use that word exactly, but I did. And liked it, as a matter of fact. "Let me keep it quick. I'm just checking out a few things. Miles' mother came to me—"

Dumb took a step toward me. "Why'd she come to you?" It was the first thing he'd spoken on his own. I was starting to get impressed.

"Can you blame her?" I figured I'd start slow and nice. My mother also said you get more flies with honey than with a sledgehammer. Okay, not exactly her words. Again. "Her son is over at the Meck getting ready to meet his maker, and she's trying anything she can to get him out. She just had some questions."

Dee's jaw jutted out slightly, hard and tense as steel, his eyes going cold as black ice. Then his voice dropped and he spoke with a precision that shocked me, like everything before was just an act. "Leave it alone."

Dumb stood there and his eyes also went to cold. I was being frosted out by a couple of fairytale characters. I wasn't quite sure what to say.

Dee continued. "We listened to her, everything she said, even if it was the mother of a murderer. It's what we do. But her son did it. End of story."

"But let me ask you, the only question I had was about the lighter."

Dee chimed in. "What about the lighter? It was his."

"But Miles said he didn't smoke."

Dee looked at me like I was stupid and laughed. "You know, you know enough of these guys, and they don't tell the truth for anything. Especially when their neck is on the line."

"Then just humor me. Miles said he didn't smoke and he said he told you that."

I could see the anger rising up in Dee's face. "I'm telling you, dick, he did it."

"But he said he didn't smoke, and the lighter wasn't his."

Dumb took it up from there. "He did it. We have two witnesses who said they've seen him smoke before, and use that lighter. Case shut."

Dee looked at me and pulled back on his coat, revealing the gun next to his hip. "I think it's time for you to leave."

How original.

I knew cops weren't really cooperative, but this was even beyond. Something was definitely starting to feel wrong about the whole case.

I felt the room behind me get a little smaller, then turned around. All the detectives had stopped what they were doing. They were turned, all of them to me, and they stared.

Right at me.

And I knew I wasn't wanted.

But that didn't stop me from wondering just what had happened to Miles along the way.

It felt like a railroad around this whole thing.

I tipped my head to the two boys, then got myself out of there.

It was one thing to poke at a hive to see what was inside. And it was a completely other, stupid thing, to keep on doing it right into their face.

I would do my poking somewhere else. It's what I was good at.

I was also good at getting to the bottom of things. The only trouble was, could I get to the bottom of it in a day and a half?

Well, I had to. For Mrs. White. And I guess Miles, too. Even though he didn't seem to care any more than I did. And that's where I always started.

Caring.

To get to the bottom of this, in a day and a half.

No pressure.

None at all.

Chapter 7

I GOT BACK TO the office and Bella was at her desk. She took one look at me, "You look like hell."

"Thanks, I appreciate the support."

I continued into my office and Bella followed me in. "You were gone long enough. You're not thinking about taking this case, are you?"

I took off my jacket and sat at my desk. I was dog tired, and felt like I could probably sleep in the chair if I wanted to. Hmm, like I did last night. "I'm thinking about it."

Bella sat down on the chair in front of me and stared directly into my eyes. She wasn't going to let me off easy. "So what are you planning on doing? You have the Crouse case. You have the Kirkman case. And Jeremy Garcia called twice this morning, wondering when you were going to let him know what's going on with his wife."

"His wife is seeing another guy."

"He already knew that."

"Well what does he want, then?"

"Exactly what you promised him. Proof. And a report." Bella

looked at me like she was a big-shot lawyer, running closing arguments against a very much losing defendant. "So when exactly were you planning on working on this new case?"

I wasn't in the mood for reality. "I suppose now. Because the guy is about to die. You know, with a rope and everything strung around his neck?" I didn't like the humor of that, but sometimes that was all you had. Especially when everything else was stacked against you. Including the person sitting right in front of you.

Bella looked at me with equal parts anger and, I supposed, compassion. She always managed to work that one in. So as much as I wanted to get mad at her, she was at least talking sense.

Sense I didn't want to admit.

She shifted in her chair and softened her gaze. She was about to pounce, and I knew it. "You can't do this alone, John."

There it was. Her classic argument. She was always wheedling to get in on everything. Not so much get in on, but... she always wanted to help. Damn her.

And she was right.

It was starting to hit me just how much I had on my plate. I had five active cases going, plus now this one.

I ran my hand over my face. "Something feels fishy about this."

"What?"

Again, she was giving me the caring. "Well, the two cops, the detectives who had the case — I call them Tweedle-Dee and Tweedle-Dumb—"

Bella laughed. "They're not the—"

"Yeah, the two bald ones."

Now she let out a noise closer to snake spitting. "I never liked them."

I eased back into my chair and closed my eyes. God I wanted to sleep. "You wouldn't like 'em much better now. Their main evidence was a lighter found at the scene. Had an *M* on it."

"Miles?"

"Or something else. Miles insists he never saw it in his life. And he doesn't smoke."

"So why are Dee and Dumb so locked on it?"

"Well, they say they have two witnesses that said it was Miles', and that the witnesses saw him use it."

"Somebody's word against somebody else's. That's about par for the course."

"I know, but… they just clammed up about anything else. And I saw something cross between the two of them."

"What?"

"A look."

Bella looked at me. She trusted me. She'd been with me too long. "So what do we do?"

There was that *we* part again. "Well, *I* am going to go over to the lawyer's. See what he has to say."

"Well, *I* don't care how much of an idiot you are—"

Bella, always sweet-talking me…

"I'm a lot smarter than answering phones and adding up invoices. Charlie, too. And if you're too stupid to use us, then it's your own funeral."

"I'll let you help. And you can start by calling everyone and letting them know that I'm working hard on their cases, and should have everything wrapped up by the day after tomorrow."

"All of them?"

"All of them."

"Bull."

"You gotta watch your language, Bella. Charlie's just a kid."

"He's no kid. And stop changing the subject. You need to take care of yourself, John — first."

"You want to tell that to Miles? Or his mother?"

"You're an idiot."

I'd been called worse.

Bella softened. Just a bit. "I don't like you like this."

"Like how?"

"Almost dead."

Yep. Made two of us.

"And if you drop dead, or dead asleep, there's no helping them anyway. So be smart." She got up from the chair. "You need us, need us to help. You're killing yourself and it's not something I like to watch."

"I appreciate it, Bella, but—"

"No buts. You think we're not smart or something? We can't handle it? Even Charlie is better than all the filing you have him doing."

It wasn't like I had a problem relying on other people, I just liked to do things myself. "This has nothing to do with either of you."

"No, it doesn't. It has everything to do with your stubbornness. If you want this agency to fail, it's up to you. But I personally need this job, and to be honest, I like it. When you're not being an ass, that is. And right now, you're being a total one."

Bella walked out and my office door came shutting behind her, leaving me alone. As always. The way I liked it.

See, that was exactly the thing, I did think I was the only one that could get it all done.

If you want something done right, you do it yourself. Then there's no one else around to… monkey it up. Or get in the way. Or…

But maybe she was right.

Maybe I did need to ask for help a little more. But that's a hard thing to do when somebody else's life is on the line. It's not something I do easily.

Hell, it's not something I do, ever.

Chapter 8

I GAVE A HALF-HEARTED attempt at two of the other cases, just to see if I could finish them in five minutes. No go.

Then a quick, soft knock sounded at my door, and the door opened behind it. Bella stood there.

She looked at me like she had a question in her eyes, and like someone had beat her with a confusion stick. But she said nothing.

I wasn't in the mood for it. "What?"

"There's a guy here to see you… from Golden Pictures."

That was odd. "Well, what does he want?"

Bella shrugged her shoulders. "I'm not sure. He wouldn't tell me."

I'd never seen her like that. It was as if the King of England had walked in, and she didn't know how to act. Probably because Hollywood had come to call. And with all of the fan magazines Bella read, it probably got her excited that a little piece of it had come into her life. She honestly looked like a little girl.

I nodded to her. "Well, send him in."

Bella stood there still for a split second, not sure what to do, even though I had given her a hint. As in — let him in.

I pointed at the door and she seemed to finally come to, and then went out.

In the next second, a man walked in my door. He was a little younger than me, probably his early thirties, light, sandy hair, short, no hat, and a suit that looked like it was worth ten times more than mine.

His face had well-defined features and eyes that seemed to be taking everything in. They went from the safes in my office to the window over on Carol, back to me, then down to my desk, as if in two and a half seconds he could see everything around him.

He was a little smaller than me and had a smile that looked like he had just stepped out of a movie. The guy extended his hand toward me. "Hi, I'm Max Whiting. Head of PR at Golden Pictures."

I stood up, took his hand, and shook it. There was something that I couldn't quite make out about him. He seemed to be happy.

I guess somebody had to be.

But for all of the smile on his face and the laughter in his eyes, there was also something a little deeper in him. I could tell he had been in the war. It's something you couldn't tell other people about, but you just knew. There was a quietness that settled inside you that came from facing death.

"Hi. John Devin." His grip was solid, and I nodded toward the two chairs in front of my desk.

He sat down and looked like he had lived in the chair forever. He was relaxed, confident, and added a little bit of energy to the room.

"So, Mr. Whiting."

His smile got even larger. "Please, just Max. Max." He shrugged his shoulders on that last *Max*, as if it didn't matter. As if trying to put me at ease.

I already was. At ease. It was my own office. "Well then — Max — why are you here?"

Max looked around and seemed to be preoccupied with my safes. I guess with seven of them, it was a little different. "Did all those come with the office?"

That was new. Usually people asked me if I was a collector. Or if I was nuts. Or I suppose maybe those two were the same. "I just like them. Some people like paintings, I like safes."

Max shrugged and kept his smile. "I'll get right to the point. I work at Golden Pictures."

"You already said that." It wasn't cutting anything for me.

"You're right. And I work for Mr. Gold himself. We've heard a rumor that you're looking into the Liliana McGann case." And he still smiled. And stopped talking, waiting for me to answer.

And I didn't.

After waiting a good twenty seconds without any reply from me, Max pushed on, his smile still intact. "Well, I suppose if you were, you couldn't tell me anyway. But I know it's true. The reason for me stopping was to find out why exactly you were looking into that?"

"Why is that of any concern to you? Or to Mr. Gold?"

Max looked off and out the window onto 7th. I supposed to collect his thoughts. Although the way he was able to talk, all golden-tongued, which was funny considering where he worked, I figured he could keep on going as long as he wanted.

The pause was probably for dramatic effect.

I'd seen that in the pictures.

"Fine, I'll be honest, Mr. Devin. Mr. Gold is releasing Liliana's last picture tomorrow. And he's hoping to not dredge up all of the old publicity about it."

"That's odd," I said. "Not wanting to dredge up the old publicity — by releasing the picture on the exact day that her convicted murderer is hanged. That doesn't make sense."

Max looked at me like I was an animal he was trying to figure out how to talk to. "The picture is a last tribute to Liliana. That's all any of this is. And Mr. Gold wondered if perhaps... you could find a way to delay your investigation until after the movie opens."

"Well, that wouldn't be too good for Miles now would it?"

"Who is Miles?"

"The guy about to be hanged. The one accused of murdering her."

"You mean who did murder her. He was convicted."

"I'll stick to my version."

"Hmm…"

I looked at him. "Don't they say that even bad publicity is good publicity?"

Max shifted in his seat. "That's what they say. But I'm not sure I believe that."

"Seems Mr. Gold was looking for exactly that, picking tomorrow to release the picture. Seems like he'll make even more money. What with the press fanning everything. Like you know they will. Because you're in PR."

Max was looking a little less smiley. "All we are trying to do is to respect Liliana."

"By opening a picture on the day her accused murderer is executed." He had a real brass pair.

"All right… all right, Mr. Devin."

"Devin. Devin is fine."

"Devin, then. I just wanted to stop over to introduce myself, maybe ask if it was possible—"

"It's not."

"And I respect that. But if it's a question of needing more work, Mr. Gold from time to time needs investigative services outside the studio. If you were in need."

His smile was mostly gone, but a little of it was still there. It was relentless.

His eyes were soft blue, and I'm sure he usually had everybody eating out of his hand.

Max got up out of the chair. "Well, Mr. Devin…"

"Just Devin."

Then he actually laughed. And the look was back on his face, confident, and the smile was even back. Like he had just stepped out of a movie. "Well then, let this just be a chance to say hello. But you can check all you want, the boy is guilty. It was proven in a court of law, the police questioned no one else, and he was convicted by a jury of his peers. It seems to me, Devin, that if you're going at this, you're not going to do anything except waste a lot of your own time."

"I guess for me, time is all I have. Because the kid doesn't have any."

I opened my office door and we walked out into the outer office.

Bella was waiting. A nice smile for the Hollywood man.

"Well, Devin," Max extended his hand, ever the polite individual, "it was nice to meet you."

I took his hand and shook it. "The same."

Max walked to the outer door, opened it, and was just about to step out, but turned back, smiling at me. "You are a tough son of a bitch, aren't you?"

I heard a choked-off laugh coming from behind me. Bella.

I smiled back at Max. "Damn right."

Max smiled and walked out, shutting the door behind him.

I turned around to Bella, who was still smiling.

Charlie, over at his card table, had the decency to face the wall. Most likely to hide his face, right above his shoulders that were jerking around. From laughing.

"Nothing, from either of you."

Then I walked back into my office and closed the door behind me.

Max was funny, but his offer wasn't.

It was too well planned. Well, not planned, it was just too convenient.

Right after I had visited Tweedle-Dee and Tweedle-Dumb.

Word got around fast.

And fast to a very specific place.

Seemed I had rattled some kind of cage. And this case was starting to get interesting.

Chapter 9

THE LAWYER'S OFFICE WAS on 5th between Hill and Broadway. The fifth floor of a six-story building. A walk-up. I was tired by the time I got to the top.

I found the office at the end of the dark hallway. A darkened hallway filled with the voice of a man shouting. "You're worthless. And if you don't do it right this time, June, I swear I will fire you — today."

The only thing I heard in response was a small woman's, maybe a girl's, voice saying "I'm sorry." Over and over, like she could somehow make it all right.

The sound of the shouting got louder the closer I got to the solid wood door of Horace P. Streck, Attorney at Law. I didn't like what was happening on the other side of it so instead of opening it nice and gentleman like, I threw it open like I meant to kill the guy on the other side.

Horace P. Streck, all of five-four with a small bowling ball of a belly, stood stooped over a small reception desk, with an even smaller, short-haired, blonde girl seated at it. His too-small, balled up fists rested on the side of the desk and his apple face tried to push itself nearly into the girl.

She had to be only eighteen and soft as a kitten. He, in his late fifties, and hard. Hard as a dried stick.

Old Horace bolted upright, like he had been caught doing something he shouldn't have. But immediately the sharp look of a hawk slammed into his eyes and, before even thinking, he opened his mouth. "Who are you?"

I walked right up to him, my six feet towering over him, and then he started to really look mad.

I looked down at the girl at the reception desk, June if I heard right from out in the hall, and I knew I had heard right. She definitely was no more than eighteen. A little older than Charlie, and getting reamed out like that.

She looked scared. Horace looked like a jackass.

I faced him and paused for a second, letting my height rub him the wrong way. "Mrs. White hired me."

Horace looked at me, a question in his eye.

"Miles White's mother," little June piped up in her small voice.

Horace sent a withering look at her. "I know who she is."

I wanted to drive my foot down into the top of his and crush it. But I didn't. It would have been fun, though. "She came to me this morning."

"Isn't he about to be hanged?"

This guy was an A-number-one peach. "That's what the state wants. His mother wants different. I thought maybe we could sit down and I could—"

"Just who are you?"

"A PI. John Devin."

"Let me see your credentials."

I looked down at June as I pulled out my wallet. She still hadn't looked back up from the spot she had decided to stare down at on the top of her desk. I felt sorry for the kid.

I flipped my wallet open to my ticket and showed it to Horace. His expression didn't change. "So what do you want?"

"Just to talk to you a bit, about the case. His mother thinks he was railroaded."

"Of course. She's a mother. Mothers do that."

My patience was wearing thing. "A couple of questions. No big problems. I'm just trying to get a handle on this."

"What handle? He was convicted. And he was guilty."

"Just a couple of minutes." I was trying to hold it in.

Horace could tell by the way I stood there that I wasn't going to leave until he talked with me. "All right. I have a meeting in five minutes. You got that much." Then he turned, walked toward the single door in the corner of the room, and then disappeared inside.

I looked down at June and smiled at her. "He always like that?"

Her cheeks got red, the way only young kids' do. Then she gave me a little smile.

"That's what I thought."

I nodded to her and touched my hand to my head, out of respect. "Time to earn my money."

And I headed into the jackass' office.

Chapter 10

INSIDE HORACE'S OFFICE, IT looked like a windstorm had met with a paper factory. There were piles of papers everywhere, and nothing looked like it was organized in any way. And that bothered me. A lot.

I wasn't necessarily the cleanest person in the world, but when other people depended on you, you did what you needed to do. There were two small sets of books along the long windowsill in back of his desk, and nothing much else that looked like a lawyer.

His desk was large and overly ornate, even filled with the piles of paper I could see that. It was like a large ship crammed into a small bathtub. A vain man's attempt at kingliness.

Horace sat in the hard black chair behind his desk and pointed at the single, cheap chair sitting in front of it. "You've got five minutes of my undivided attention."

I doubted it. "I went up to visit Miles at the Meck."

Horace looked at me like he didn't think I was telling the truth. "He seemed innocent to me."

Horace laughed, a thin, high laugh. Like a girl. "I don't know why you're wasting your time on this. He was convicted, and he was sentenced to death."

It seemed like that was all that Horace could ever say. "I like to think maybe he's being honest, and that maybe he's innocent. What do you think?"

Horace absently picked up a pencil and started doodling on a piece of blank white paper. The pencil never stopped. "I took the case because of his high profile. I thought why not, everyone deserves a chance."

It didn't seem like Horace believed that to me.

"You have talked to the police, right?"

I like to let people think they are the only ones supplying me with information. "No, that was my next stop."

"Well, you should've saved yourself the trouble and gone there first. It was open and shut." He waved his hand as if he was shooing away a fly. "They caught him drunk there at the scene, passed out. Completely passed out. It was an open-and-shut case and there was nothing I could have done."

"But see, that's a question I have."

Horace looked at me with sharp, dark eyes. I could tell he didn't like to be questioned. At all. "When I talked with Miles, the one thing that didn't add up was he kept saying that he didn't smoke."

Horace got angry, a little more angry than he should have. "The lighter? We have direct testimony from two witnesses that said not only that he smoked, but that they saw him with that exact lighter."

He was sounding like a regular district attorney, not like someone who was supposed to have defended Miles. "But that's just the thing. Miles kept telling you that he didn't smoke, and that he had never seen that lighter in his life. But he said that you kept dismissing that. Why was that?"

Horace stood up from behind his desk like a shot, and his face had already gone red. Anger red. "Like I told you, Mr. Devin, I defended him completely and utterly." Then he walked over to the door to his office and opened it. "Now if you wouldn't mind, I have to prepare for my next meeting." It looked like orders from a teacher. A teacher who knew that the student was bigger than him and would probably pound him into the ground. Unlike the girl out front at the desk. Who *he* had no problems pounding into the ground.

Bullies were the same everywhere. "Why don't you just sit back down, Horace."

The look on his face was priceless. Like he'd never been talked to that way.

"I will call the police."

I smiled. "I'd be glad if you did. But there's a couple of things I want to say first. When Miles' mother walked in and asked me to look into this, I thought she was grabbing at straws. So I went up to talk with Miles, just to relieve my mind. I like to do that when somebody's life is on the line. Because, for some reason, I started to believe her. Even just a little bit. So when I got to talk with Miles and he told me about that lighter, and that you didn't even pursue it—"

"I pursued everything. And if you are accusing me of not representing my client to my fullest—"

"I didn't say a thing, Horace. You just did."

"Get out."

"I just asked a question about a lighter."

"I said get out."

"I want to see his file, everything you have on the case."

Horace got a tight smirk on his face. "That is privileged information with my client, and my client alone."

He was right, I had no ability to get the file. But I tried something just for the heck of it. "His mother paid you, didn't she?"

Horace stopped short.

"She's the one who hired you to represent Miles, am I right?"

Horace looked at me like he was trying to figure out what I wanted.

He was even slower than I thought. "Since she hired you, she's your client. I'll have her phone over and have her release the files to me."

Horace smiled, not a nice smile at all. "Of course. Have her call me. Then I'll give you the file."

I got up from the chair and walked past him, and I towered over him as I did. I liked that. "Have a nice day, Horace."

Horace shut the door on me.

Even before I was out of his office.

Ass.

Chapter 11

JUNE LOOKED UP AT me quick as the door slammed behind me, then back down to her usual spot on the desk. It must be something really interesting.

"So he *is* always like that."

She looked out the corner of her eye at the closed door behind me. No one could see her. Well, specifically, Horace couldn't see her. She nodded her head.

"My condolences." I smiled at her and she actually looked over to take it.

And she smiled back.

It looked good on her. She seemed like a good kid in the wrong spot. "You should think about working somewhere else."

She looked up at me and she had young blue eyes. Innocent ones that definitely didn't deserve to be putting up with what she did. But I understood. The way things were, you held on to a job any way you could. Even if it was eating away at you.

White knuckles. That's how I called it. What you had to do to hold on to anything in this Depression.

"By the way, my name is Devin." I extended my hand to her.

She looked at me like I was from some other planet. Which would make sense, because around here she wasn't exactly treated nice. Then she shocked me and took it. My hand. She was tentative, but she was learning. "June. My name is June."

She tucked a piece of hair that wasn't out of place back in behind her ear.

I kept up my smile; I figured she could use it. "I hope you don't mind, and hopefully Horace doesn't come out, but could I use your phone? I need to ask my secretary if she could call Miles' mother. You know, Mrs. White? I'm guessing you heard in there, but Horace doesn't want to give me the file. Which is okay, I understand. But Miles is about to go to the gallows and I promised his mother that I'd try anything I could to see if I could make that not happen. I just need my secretary to call her and ask her to call back here with permission, so that Horace in there will give me the file. Is that okay?"

June looked over at the closed door with Horace on the other side. I'm sure she was afraid he was going to come out at any minute. But she turned back to me. "What's the number?"

Brave kid.

I gave June the number to my office, and she dialed.

The thing about a phone is it's not too private, especially when it's at someone else's desk. Bella answered. "Hey Bella, it's me."

"Where are you at?"

"Still at the lawyer's office. He's a real piece of work."

June smiled. Apparently she liked when someone was thinking along the same line as her.

"Call Mrs. White and ask her to call over here." I looked down at June. "What's the number here?"

"Tyler-478."

"Did you hear that, Bella?"

"I heard it."

"Good. Have her give a call here and talk to June. Don't ask for the lawyer, ask for June. She'll treat her nice." I smiled at June.

"So you're finally going to let me do something on this one?"

I raised my eyebrows to June. "Don't give me any lip."

"I'll do it right away, *sir.*" Bella laughed and hung up.

I smiled at June. "She's actually the one who tells me what to do."

June smiled.

It was a good smile.

I hoped for her; she could use it a little more often.

Chapter 12

I WAS ALREADY DOWNTOWN so I swung by the LA Guardian Building.

The oldest paper in LA, the Guardian had an archive on the city a mile long. Well, not a mile, just a huge basement that held all their newspapers, stories, story notes, and the main thing that I was looking for — photos.

Plus, I knew a guy.

Everything just came back to the lighter and I didn't know why. It kept gnawing at me. It was such a small thing and it made absolutely no sense.

It wasn't Miles', at least according to him. And I believed him. But whose was it?

It was as if this one small thing had started a huge chain, which now hung around Miles' neck. Find a lighter, it has an *M* on it, so it must be Miles'.

But it wasn't.

It was as if they all wanted the case to be solved fast, the trial to be done fast. It was as if they wanted him to be guilty.

So who did the lighter really belong to?

It took me fifteen minutes and a five-dollar bill handed over, and I had a dupe made of the photo of the lighter.

It was a simple thing, with a large *M* engraved in the middle of it, and a circle of fancy scrollwork engraved around it. Like something from out of an Italian painting. Or something.

Next up it was Cardon. I had to talk with him, but I didn't want to see him in the detective room. Too many questions from Dee and Dumb. But there was one thing predictable about Cardon, especially by the afternoon.

Across the street from police headquarters was a small diner. Nothing to speak of. Inside, the food wasn't great, the coffee was even worse, but it was somewhere other than the detectives' room at LA police headquarters. And Cardon was always there by the afternoon.

He had been a detective for a few years. He had started up in the Valley and now was headquartered downtown in City Hall.

I don't know why, but he had never settled with a partner. Or maybe they had never settled with him. Cardon tended to be a little quiet and a lot honest. Up in the Valley he had blown the whistle on a couple of cops. Not really blew the whistle, he had tried to handle things quiet when he found out they had been on the take for more than a little while. Handle things quiet, handle things easy — and he ended up getting frozen out. By a lot of people. But he was a damned good detective and ended up transferring downtown.

And still, nobody had wanted him as a partner.

I guess that's why we hit it off. We both liked to work alone.

Except when I needed him.

The Schenectady Diner had three windows along the front of the place, and one along the side. The three front windows faced out onto City Hall where the detectives were located. Finished not that long ago, the tall, white granite building jutted almost five hundred feet and definitely thirty-two stories out of the center of downtown Los Angeles, and called out to the rest of the world that the city was here. Inside the building was corruption and people wanting to do good. Lawyers and politicians, detectives and grunts, everyone working for what they thought was right, whether what was right was legal, illegal, or — most of the time — somewhere in between.

There were only five people in the diner, spread out with two at the counter, two in one booth, and Cardon, in the back as usual at his small chromium-edged table. Away from the window and with his back to the wall. An honest, quiet cowboy, out to do good. In a place bordering on very, very bad.

The green-topped table was covered for the most part by scattered papers and files, a three-quarters-empty heavy white coffee cup, and a couple of almost-used-up pencils. Cardon leaned over everything, a man peacefully digging out a buried locomotive with a toothpick.

"Cardon."

He looked up, surprise in his sharp eyes. "Devin. I thought you were off saving somebody from being hanged."

I smiled and sat down at the chair opposite him, careful not to muss his business. "I am, actually."

Then Cardon's eyes went just a little more narrow, like he didn't want to see me. It was a smart look.

"Do you remember back to the case?"

Cardon didn't like where this was headed. "Yeah… and just why are you here talking with me?"

"See, that's what I like about you Cardon, you're a good detective. And yes, you can help me."

"You didn't ask me anything."

"I am now."

Cardon smiled a small, thin smile, then picked up all his papers and folders and stuffed them into a small black case, threw a dollar down on the tabletop, and headed to the door.

I chased after him. I wasn't afraid to beg.

He was pretty quick for a small guy, and I finally managed to stop him outside the diner door. "Come on, Cardon, you got to help me on this one."

"I don't have to help you with anything." Then he looked angry, nodding down at his black case. "Do you even know how much I have to do here? It's just me, I have no one else. Me." Then he looked straight into my eyes. His soft hazel eyes were sharp, and trying to push me away. "Because I already know what's coming."

"Oh you do?"

"Yes I do."

"Like I say, you're a really good detective… Detective Cardon." And then I threw in a smile. To disarm him.

The sun hit both of us as we stood there out on the sidewalk, LA City Hall beyond us. It was a standoff.

We looked at each other as someone cut behind us to go into the diner. I hoped it wasn't another detective. "Cardon, there are some things that just don't make any sense."

"What are you even doing on this case? I mean, they're hanging him tomorrow." But I could tell from his look that he knew exactly why I was on this.

"See," I smiled even bigger, "that's where you have it wrong." I nodded down at my strap watch. "It's actually tomorrow at midnight. So more than a whole day."

He looked like a parent who was caving in. "You know what I mean."

"I know what you mean. And I know I'm asking for a lot."

"Again, I reiterate, you haven't even asked for anything. And I like it exactly that way."

"Price and Black, what do you think of them?"

Cardon dropped his eyes down to his shoes, then looked out into the street, then looked up at the sun.

"I hope you don't go blind."

"All right. They're two detectives I work with. You don't want to know anything else."

"That's exactly what I was thinking. It just doesn't add up. I think they may be covering something up."

Cardon laughed. "That's melodramatic."

"It's the truth."

Cardon didn't say anything more, but I could tell he knew what I was talking about. He didn't have someone else's hand in his pocket.

"Here's what I'm hoping, Cardon — just check a couple of things in the file. I know I can't take a look at it, but you can. It's all I'm asking."

"And what am I supposed to do with my cases that I've got now? What do you want me to tell the family of the guy that was just killed up in Los Feliz?"

I shrugged my shoulders. "Tell them you're trying to keep another guy alive." I didn't know what else to tell him. There was really nothing else to tell him. "It's just a feeling I have." And that was as honest as I could be.

Cardon squinted his eyes at me, and I don't think it was because of the sun. Then he let out a long, shallow sigh. "What you want me to check?"

I was tired, I was about dead, and it was the best thing I'd heard in a couple of days. "Miles told me about the lighter, the lighter they found with film. It sounds simple, and way too easy, but Miles said he didn't smoke."

Anger started to seep back into Cardon's eyes. "People accused of murder often say things that aren't true. I thought you were better than that."

I was bone tired, and I was tired of all of this. I had too much to do with all of the other cases I had, and already I knew, so much to do with this one. I just needed a little bit of help. "I don't know, I just believe him. Price and Black said that Liliana's business partners said that he smoked. I'm about to head over to talk with them, and I'm sure they'll tell me the same thing, but from what I hear about them, they don't seem like the most up-and-up people on the face of the planet. And they're the only ones saying it. His mother even says it. He didn't smoke."

"So I'm asking you again, what are you asking me to check?"

"Just look into the file. See if they followed up on all the leads. See if they followed up everything, the way you would follow up on everything." Cardon started to open his mouth but I rode right over him. "And yeah, I know, nobody would follow up things like you. But it's like they found the lighter, and that was that. It all stopped. And even Miles' lawyer stopped him, as soon as Miles brought up the lighter. It's like all of them wrapped onto that lighter and ran with it. And nobody would listen to anything else. Like they avoided everything else. Like they railroaded the guy."

Cardon shifted his briefcase from one hand to the other, either a little nervous, or just to do something.

Then he nodded, crossed the street, and headed to the great white tower of City Hall.

I don't know what I was hoping he would find, but I was hoping there was something. Maybe even confirmation that the little feeling I had in the back of my head was right.

I headed to my car.

It was time to talk to those business partners of Liliana. Although I doubted I would get anything.

Unless I hit them. Then I would get something.

And at that point, it sounded kind of fun.

Chapter 13

NEXT UP WAS THE business partners.

From what Miles had said, they were both pieces of work. Together, and separately.

The restaurant they owned with Liliana was located at the far east end of Hollywood. Which pretty much wasn't even in Hollywood anymore.

The restaurant was called the Moroccan Nights and as I drove up it looked, well… Moroccan.

Located on a corner facing out onto Hollywood Boulevard, it was surrounded with high, white walls with the main part of the restaurant rising up from inside.

I aimed my car at a huge stone lacework arch cut into the wall and drove into the place.

Inside was a true Moroccan sultan's palace. A flat roof, the building all in white stucco, three stories tall, with more stone lacework arches along the front of it. Peaked windows were cut along the face of the building, with small white lights in the shape of palm trees bolted on either side of the massive front doors.

The building itself was arranged in an *L* shape with the long part facing out toward Hollywood Boulevard, and a fountain sat in front of everything with no water coming from it. It was dry. And dead, from the looks of it. As was the rest of the place.

The courtyard itself was made up of a pattern of light and dark red bricks, and there were only two cars parked on it. My car would make three.

I drove around the fountain to almost in front of the place and parked.

The place had cost a lot, from the looks of it, but looked sad with no one there. Like a reflection of Liliana's death.

I'd heard it wasn't doing too well after she died.

Now I'm sure, for the first six months after, the place was hopping. Hollywood was nothing if not a celebrator of the rising and the gone. But with the way things always go, there were other risers, and others fallen, who had already more than taken Liliana's place.

I walked under a great arch at the inside of the corner of the *L*-shape of the building and headed for the front door.

Made of rough sawn wood that looked like it belonged protecting some Arabian palace of five hundred years ago, the door had a large, long, twisting piece of black wrought iron that I guess served as the door pull. I pulled it, and the great door opened.

Inside it was like the inside of a harem. Or at least what I thought a harem should look like. A lobby, with red silk panels hanging from a twenty-foot-tall ceiling, and a deep red and cream carpet below, spread out in front of me. Exotic tapestries hung from every wall, and if what I could make out of them was right, a lot had scenes of men and woman doing… what men and women do.

I almost blushed.

An odd thing for an ex-Marine, but there you have it.

Ahead, standing at a small podium of light wood, edged with the same Arabian lacework I saw in the arches outside, stood a guy.

I'm guessing some kind of a maître d', he was short and wore a red turban that looked like it was falling off his head. He had a small chest, a bit of a belly, loose pants, small eyes, and honest to God looked like he was from Jersey. He opened his thin mouth like a pimp trying to drum up business for a girl. "Do you have a reservation?"

I almost laughed. Sure enough, a Jersey accent. Sometimes I amaze myself. "I'm here to see Daisy and James."

"You looking for money?"

Straight to the point. Apparently the look of death outside carried inside. "No money, just a couple of questions. About Liliana."

He cocked his head and looked out at me from one eye. "You a cop?"

"No."

"A newspaper guy?"

"No. A PI."

Then he twisted his head back and looked at me with both eyes. "Really?"

"Really."

"I was thinking of getting into that racket. I'm here between jobs."

The Sultan adjusted his turban. I guess finally wanting to look like something. It didn't work.

I looked around the place. Over to the right was a small sitting area and, from there, a corner that led to some other part of the place. Into the small part of the *L* of the building.

To my left was the long, empty dining room. If the lobby was what I thought was a harem, the dining room really was. It was done in pinks, greens, and creams, high-backed chairs, table cloths, and enough silk on the walls and hanging from the ceiling to make underwear for 40,000 women.

At least, I thought.

I turned back to the Sultan of Jersey. "Like I say, can you tell me where Daisy and James are?"

Just then a large bunch of indiscriminate yelling came from around the corner to the right. Over from the small part of the building.

A man's and a woman's voice. The woman's voice was high and screeching, the man's low like a cannon.

The screecher questioned the relation of the other person to his mother, while the other person, the cannon of the two, shot declarations about the woman's copious relations with… as far as I could tell… the rest of the world.

The Sultan of Jersey sighed, "You want Dick and Jane?" and nodded to the corner to my right. And whatever was fighting in the short part of the building.

I girded my loins.

And headed for the excitement.

Chapter 14

INSIDE THE SMALLER PART of that *L* was a hall that led to a lounge.

In the hall, the twenty-foot ceilings from the lobby gave way to more great pieces of silk hanging down, even lower, from the ceiling. It was completely red now, the ceiling and the walls, and created a very close feeling leading to the lounge's entry.

I suppose it was meant to be nice, but it wasn't. It just made you feel like you wanted to get out of there. Especially with the yelling coming from the lounge on the other side.

The lounge itself was relatively small and, overall, overpowering.

And pretty open for a place that served liquor during Prohibition.

The bar itself was located to the left, and there were all kinds of bottles of beautiful liquids running along the back of it. A big, thick guy, in the same kind of red turban the Sultan sported out front, stood behind the long bar and stared at me. Maybe he didn't like strangers.

In front of him sat the rest of the lounge with small circle-topped tables scattered around, while underneath was a huge carpet of red and cream curls and swords that I suppose was meant to look like Arabia.

One massive blue hookah pipe sat to the right as I walked in. It looked like it had been made in Jersey.

I wondered if the Sultan had brought it with him.

"Get away from me!" That was the screecher, from somewhere in the back deep darkness of the place. It was funny how the voice cut through the great heaviness of the room.

"Who are *you?*"

That last was directed at me, from a man who walked out of the deep darkness followed by a dame.

She had platinum white hair, dirty and curled, and a tight sunken face that looked like it was something five years ago. Daisy, I guessed. She really did have a few miles under her belt. Not that her lungs knew about it. "Who did you invite?!" That was to the guy, then she turned her look at me. "We don't want any!"

The bartender just kept standing. He looked like he was letting them tire themselves out. And from the resignation in his face, he looked like he did it often.

"I'm not selling anything. I'm a PI, and I just had a couple of questions—"

"Who do you work for?" The man came up to me.

James. According to Miles, a former director who hadn't directed in more than a few years, but played off those three pictures like an old, broken soldier lived off former dreams.

"A Mrs. White."

"Who's White?"

James was in my face now. He stood a little shorter had a drooping face, the smell of whiskey on his breath, and a head going just bald. But he covered it well. The bald spot. I figured he could give a damn about the whiskey.

"Mother to Miles White."

It took James a bit, but a lightbulb went off through the haze in his eyes and those same eyes tightened, and his body followed suit. "She at it again?"

"What do you mean?"

Daisy piped up. "She still trying to prove the kid didn't do it?" There was a hardness to her, and her body tightened to complete stillness. Very controlled. She smiled. "Funny, I thought the kid was already dead for it."

I didn't like her before I met her. Now I really didn't like her at all. "Not till tomorrow. So you're close."

Daisy looked at James. "See, I'm close. There's at least something I did right today."

"Let me just ask a couple questions and I'll let you get back to whatever it was you were doing."

James laughed. "You mean wishing I was dead?"

Daisy slugged him in the shoulder. "Shut up." Then she turned to me. "What do you want?"

Honestly, I wanted out of there. "You all went to the Papaya Room that night, didn't you?"

James sat down on one of the silk-topped, blue stools at the bar and lit a cigarette. "We did."

"And you all got along well?"

Daisy snorted. "We all hated each other. At least most of the time. But we still drank together."

"You can't stop the drinking." James' eyes went soft, like he was talking about an old and dear girlfriend.

"You hated each other, but you drank together?"

Daisy looked at me like I was nuts. Or actually, more like a child who couldn't understand how the world really worked. "'Course we did. At least twice a week. Usually at the Papaya Room. It's just the way things worked. You stay with your friends."

From the sounds of all of them, I didn't know how good of friends they were. And if those were Liliana's friends, she was crazy for staying with them. Of course, that's what she got in the end. "So, who was usually there?"

She looked over at James, nodded at him. "Well, him. Of course. Always him." Her eyes had gone to ice, and she stabbed him with them. "Go ahead, tell him why you were always there. Always with her." Then Daisy looked back at me. "Those two were an item."

James dropped his eyes down. "It was only twice."

Daisy smiled. "Two times — times five more." Then she looked at me. "The PI I hired found those two together at least ten times. But who's counting?"

"You are, dear."

I got the feeling this was all normal for them, like breathing. Like what they did for marriage. And if that was Hollywood, you could keep it. "So, who was there that night?"

Daisy shrugged her shoulders. "Who wasn't? There was he and I, Louis Gold, Dante Manzione, and a few other people. Mostly from the studio side. Gold never went anywhere alone."

"What was talked about that night?"

She laughed. "Oh, not much, just how Liliana wanted to kill all of us."

"Okay…"

"Oh, she was always a doll, a real peach, never a time when she wasn't angry. So she came into the bar that night like a train on fire. I think she had had it with everybody. She told Dante that he couldn't use the restaurant. Told him to get his stuff out of here by the next day."

"What stuff?"

She looked at me. "Are you a kid or something?"

I looked back at her with no clue what she was talking about. "Sure. Why don't you treat me like one, and explain."

"Dante had a gambling operation up on the third floor."

James winced.

Daisy faced him. "What? You don't like the truth? I like it now. Makes a lot of things a lot more clear." Then she faced me. "He ran a gambling operation up there on the third floor. We weren't using it, it was all storage. So he asked and we all said yes. It was a nice dime for the three of us. Then Liliana got all crazy about it that night and wanted him out. I tried to talk her out of it right there." She nodded to James. "He did, too. But Liliana wasn't having any of it."

I knew a little bit about Dante, and from what I'd heard, he wasn't the type to let that go. "Are you saying he killed her?"

"What are you asking? They have Miles for it."

"Could Dante have done it?"

"You got a death wish?"

I really didn't, but I liked asking questions. It helped to find the truth. "Could he?"

Daisy was on a roll. Apparently truth agreed with her. "He might have. He could have. But I think it really was the kid."

"Miles?"

"Yeah. He was the one causing all the trouble."

"How?"

"Because I think she actually felt something for him." She looked over at James. "The first time she actually felt something. We sat down here, maybe a week before she died, before she was killed. She was almost crying."

"Why?"

"Because she realized she liked the kid. More than any other person around."

"And that was a problem?"

"Because she was a mess. She was making a lot of money, sure, but Dante had her on pills. Gold was milking her for everything he could. And then there was Romeo here, who could never make up his mind. Whether to choose her or *me*, his wife."

"What did she say, exactly, that night?"

"About the kid?"

"No, at the Papaya Room. You said she wanted to kill all of you."

"Right. She was going to leave Gold, even though she had a contract. That she wanted Dante out of the third floor. And that she wanted out of this place."

"Sounds like she wanted to change everything."

Daisy smiled. A sharp smile. "She hated this place from the first. And hated Dante for starting her on the pills. But you didn't know that one, did you?"

I didn't. I just shook my head.

"And Gold, she told me a week before she wanted a new contract from him. She said she had him over a barrel. Said he was having financial problems and since she was the hottest ticket on the lot, she'd be able to name her own price. She was tired of being used."

"And what was her price?"

"Half of everything that her movies brought in."

"That's a lot."

"You ain't whistling Dixie."

I threw her a curve ball. "Did you kill her?"

Daisy looked at me, shocked. "What?"

"Did you kill Liliana?"

She looked at James and then laughed like a hyena. "There were all sorts of reasons why I wanted to kill her. But did I? No. I liked the money she brought in. It suited me."

Curve ball two. "What about the lighter?"

Instantly, something shifted in the room and a small look passed between Daisy and James.

Neither said anything, so I thought I should. "Miles said he didn't smoke."

Daisy looked at me straight in the eyes and didn't let hers leave mine. "He did."

It was a lie. I could feel it off her. And the way her body went even more rigid told me I was right.

I looked over at James. "What about you? Did Miles smoke?"

He didn't even look at me. Kept his eyes pointed down at the red and cream carpet and then walked out.

I looked at Daisy. "I think he has a problem with that question, don't you?"

Her eyes dug into me. I knew what James felt like now. It wasn't nice. "Miles smoked, it was his lighter, end of the story."

And apparently it was, because Daisy took off after James.

I watched her walk past the huge blue hookah and disappear into the thick red hallway.

I was left alone with the bartender with the red turban, and I realized he hadn't said a word the entire time.

I looked at him. "They always like this?"

He nodded, and still no words.

I wasn't getting anything from anybody around there. But I had, really.

They were lying, of course. About the lighter.

But they didn't seem like they were covering up for anything they had done. I think the only thing they were capable of was making each other's lives hell.

Now I just had to figure who they were covering for.

Fast.

Chapter 15

BELLA WALKED DOWN THE deserted hallway and she could hear the yelling from a long distance off. The closer she got to the office of Horace P. Streck, Attorney at Law, the more the haranguing resolved itself down into a single word at the end of a very long sentence. "…worthless!"

Then the door at the end of the hallway flew open, and out walked a short man with small hands, slamming the door behind him.

He walked in a black cloud straight down the hall toward Bella. She gave him a wide berth. Mostly because she didn't want to hit the guy.

And she would have.

She had five brothers, all of them older, most of them bigger, and she had learned a few things about surviving. But looking at the angry, smallness of the man as he passed, Bella decided he just wasn't worth it.

It had to be Streck. At least from the way Devin had described him.

Bella found herself at the last door at the end of the hall and opened it.

To a young girl crying.

The girl was like Devin had said. Eighteen probably, or maybe even less, with short blonde hair.

Bella smiled. "June?"

The girl quickly wiped away the tears from both her cheeks, then tried a smile. Then she completely broke down.

"Oh, come here…" Bella walked over to the desk and put an arm around June and held her. "It is June, right?"

The girl nodded.

This kind of thing ripped Bella apart. "You want me to kill him?"

June snorted a small laugh, and Bella thought that was at least progress. Then Bella pulled a handkerchief from her purse and offered it to the girl.

June took it and blew. "Thanks."

The voice came out as a slight squeak. This girl needed lessons in life. "Maybe you need to kill him yourself." Bella thought back to all she had learned. And you tend to learn a lot when your mother dies giving birth to you. Not then, but everything that comes after. "It'd do you some good."

June looked up at Bella, her eyes still damp. "Do I know you?"

Bella laughed. "Oh, sorry." She smiled at June, hopefully warmly enough. "My boss, John Devin, was here earlier. He told me your name, said you were very helpful, and I've come—"

"Yes, for the file." June got herself together, something to at least do instead of cry. Then she walked into what Bella assumed was Streck's office.

A file cabinet drawer rolled open in the other office as Bella looked down at the girl's desk. Nice and neat, and there wasn't a speck of dust anywhere. Just a blank pad of paper and a pencil. Ready for anything. There was also a small, framed photo of a baby. A very young one.

No other family photos but that, and Bella wondered if the baby was hers.

Bella called out. "He's an ass, you know."

June came out of the office holding a file. "I'm sorry?"

Bella turned to face her. "Your boss. He's a horse's ass."

June smiled a little, then tried to hide it. Then she handed Bella the file, still not looking at her.

Bella took the file, and it was thin. Way too thin for a lawyer's notes on a murder trial. "That's it?"

June still hadn't looked up at Bella. "That's all that's in the file."

Interesting choice of words, Bella thought. "A capital murder trial, and this is all he has."

"Yes, ma'am." June softly moved around Bella to sit back at her desk. Her eyes were now focused on the top of the desk.

June's jaw worked just a bit, like she wanted to say more. Or was just trying to keep herself occupied so that she didn't.

Bella figured there had to be more to the file, it just wasn't in the file itself. But judging from the guy who just left the place, it wasn't June's call. It was Streck's.

"Okay…" Bella opened the file and looked inside.

There were a few pages of handwritten notes, a summary of the trial notes, a photo of a lighter with a round circle with an *M* inside, and that was it. Nothing more. Empty, as far as Bella was concerned. "And you're sure there's not anything else?"

June still hadn't looked up. "That's all Mr. Streck gave me."

Bella doubted that she'd get anything more out of June. But you never knew unless you tried. As long as she was smart about it. She nodded her head toward the photo of the baby. "Yours?"

June looked up at Bella, then at the photo. And she smiled. Actually smiled. "Yes."

"How fresh?"

June looked up at Bella, a question in her face.

Bella laughed. It's one thing she'd learned in life: jokes break ice. Something Devin needed to learn. Because he just broke everything else. "I'm just trying to be funny. How old is the baby?"

June laughed. And smiled at the photo. "Eight months."

It wasn't exactly a novel, but at least Bella had June talking.

"Boy or girl?"

The girl looked at the photo a little longer. "Boy." Her smile got even warmer. "His name is Daryl."

"Nice kid." Bella looked at her. She seemed like a smart girl. "After the father?"

June's face went immediately blank, her voice tight. "After my father."

Okay. That went well. "I seem to have stuck my foot in it, haven't I?"

June let out a big sigh. "I'm sorry."

"Look…" Bella waited until June actually looked her in the eye. "You have nothing to be sorry for, June."

Then June's face seemed to soften, just a bit. Like she was the girl she really was. "Mr. Streck has me all angry."

"Why don't you get a different job?" Bella knew it was a stupid question, even as she asked it. Anyone who could hold a job nowadays would kill in order to keep it. Bella certainly had hers and was very lucky to have it. For a lot of other people, it wasn't so easy.

"I got this job through an uncle. He knows Mr. Streck. And it was the only thing I could get."

Bella felt sorry. "Are you at least checking for anything else?"

June shrugged her shoulders. "I don't have any time. As soon as I leave here, I head home and take Daryl from my mother. She does cleaning seven days a week."

"My boss can be an ass sometimes," Bella smiled, "But he's pretty straight. I'm lucky to have him."

June smiled. "He was nice."

"Oh, don't let that fool you. He can be a grouch. A lot, actually." Bella said it with a smile, and enough of a laugh that it brought a bigger smile out of June.

"Now let me tell you something, one secretary to another. I'm guessing Mr. Streck probably told you not to give us everything."

June didn't answer. She didn't need to.

"I can't ask you to risk your job. But the man that they

convicted, Miles White, they're going to hang him for murder. Tomorrow. Now we have no idea if he's innocent, although my boss seems to think so. God knows why. But I tend to believe Devin, even when I don't want to. He's good at what he does. But if you're able to talk to him, Mr. Streck, and get him to give us everything that's supposed to be in that file — you might be saving somebody's life."

Bella wasn't sure if she was getting to June or not.

Then she looked at the photo on June's desk.

"It was interesting. Miles' mother, Mrs. White, she came in to see Devin this morning. She's worked this whole year to try to get Miles released. We're the last detective agency she could find, and she came to us. Because she wasn't giving up. She believes Miles is innocent, and there was no stopping her." Bella nodded toward the photo of the small baby to June's side. "I guess you could understand. Only mothers can understand. What you would go through to save a child."

June said nothing.

Bella reached her hand down and put it on top of June's. "I know you're scared; and this has nothing to do with the file, but if you can, get out of here. Streck is not a nice man. You're young enough that you may not know that, or that you think it's okay. It's not. He can only hurt you."

Bella saw a lot of herself in June, but she'd lived a lot of miles between then and where she was now. Bella didn't put up with anything anymore from anyone.

And she hoped June would learn the same.

Bella took the file and left.

There was still a guy to save and, for the first time, Bella thought that maybe Devin was right.

So she headed back to the office to do whatever she could about it.

Chapter 16

LITTLE PETE'S RESTAURANT WAS an Italian place. The way Sicily was Italian. Meaning — nothing else existed.

Located east of downtown on Broadway, Little Pete's was the center of the Italian community in Los Angeles and had been for a while. But now it was known as the center of Dante Manzione's world, which meant it was the center of the Italian mob. It was the ground floor of what used to be a hotel more years ago than I'd been alive, with the upper floors serving as home for Dante's "businesses."

Dante was from back east and had worked with the mob there until he moved to LA ten years ago. At least that was the story. But what I'd found with stories, especially ones that came from the street, was that they were usually true.

The story was, he was raised in New York and came into his own at seventeen.

He'd shined shoes for a living up until that point, that point being the night he went to his first craps game and came out with $200 in his pocket. And he never looked back.

Now he was here in LA and running whatever part of the

gambling, prostitution, and dope business that wasn't already owned by Jim Nolan. Jim ran the System — LA's biggest organized crime organization. A little competition between the two.

So all in all, Dante had done good for himself. If you thought all that stuff was good.

Inside, Little Pete's was tight, closed, and full of smoke. Cigar and cigarette, to be specific. The air was blue with it.

Tables were scattered around the place, with booths along two of the walls and a bar along the third wall to my left. The tables had some people at them, a few, regulars from the looks of them, but as I looked around I also spotted at least seven of Dante's men. In suits and ties, they were big and brawny and I knew every one of them would be packing.

Even the short old bartender in a white apron who stood behind the bar, he'd be packing. He looked to be about seventy if he was a day. He had gray hair cut short, a thin face, and an eye that caught me as soon as I entered the joint. My guess was he had a shotgun behind the bar with him. Or two. Or maybe even three.

It seemed that almost everything in the place was red. Simple bentwood chairs with red seat cushions, dark red tablecloths, the carpet, the booths along the walls, even the chairs at the bar — everything was red. At least everything that wasn't dark wood.

A few forks and knives clinked to plates as I walked in, and the heavy smell of pasta and tomato sauce wrapped around me. And roast. Somewhere deep inside, a roast was in the oven.

Then I was stopped. By a Neanderthal.

An Italian one to be specific, complete with shoulders the size of a cross-beam, tiny ears, olive skin, a smashed nose, and a forehead sticking out like it was trying to keep rain off a pair of lazy brown eyes the size of quarters. I wasn't sure if the eyes were lazy because of the forehead above getting hit a lot, or it was just the way he was born. A human battering ram that was just plain battered.

The Neanderthal put his hand on my chest.

Now normally this ex-Marine wouldn't allow anybody to do

that. But seeing as how I was in Little Pete's, the home of Dante and the Italian mob in LA, I thought I'd let him do what he wanted. For now.

"I'm here to see Dante."

I looked over in the corner booth and there sat Dante, alone. A small guy in his late forties, he was trim, and had dark hair that was cut high on the side of his head. He wore a plain white shirt under his jacket with a straight black tie tied up straight and neat and tight. It was like the tie held everything about him together, straight up to his face that looked just as neat, just as tight.

The Neanderthal in front of me didn't say a word. He just stood looking at me, his wide eyes not even questioning. Just there.

"I'm asking nice. I'm not here to hurt anybody. See, I even let left my guns at home." I reached for the sides of my jacket and opened them slowly, revealing nothing underneath.

The Neanderthal reached around my back, did a quick pat-down and at least was satisfied that I wasn't there to kill everybody in the place. At least for now. But he still stayed silent. It was starting to bother me. You ever talk to a wall? It isn't pleasant.

"If you would please… if you would please be so kind… I'm asking to talk to Dante for just a couple of minutes. It's about Liliana McGann. I'm John Devin, a PI."

That at least got a reaction from the Neanderthal. At the mention of Liliana's name, he tipped his head to the side, like he was looking at something he couldn't quite understand.

Then, amazingly, he walked over to Dante.

Looking around the place, I wasn't sure why Italians loved red. Maybe it was the tomatoes. Maybe it was the wine. It just made me want to be out in the sunshine again.

The Neanderthal made it over to Dante and leaned over to talk into his ear.

They traded a few words back and forth and Dante looked up at me with a tipped head just like the Neanderthal. I liked to think it wasn't about me, but about Liliana. She was dead. But the case wasn't. At least as far as I was concerned.

Dante went back to his lunch and the Neanderthal headed back toward me. When he got back to me, his eyebrows came together like they were really, and I mean really, working hard. "Okay."

That's all he said.

But he got it together enough to nod behind him, in Dante's direction.

I took that to mean that I was clear to walk, so I did. Apparently I got an audience with Dante. The Neanderthal stayed by the door. I supposed to keep out the rabble, which actually should have included me.

Dante sat alone at his booth. Except for the three guys standing behind the booth. All goons in dark suits, all with close-cut hair, all with looks like they wanted to let me know they'd love to kill me if I gave them even a quarter chance.

A regular welcoming committee.

Dante looked up at me, a plate of some kind of fish in front of him.

Dante didn't smile and I heard he never did. His left eye was sharp and his right eye drooped, something about a beating he took back east. And another mark of that was a scar that trailed down from his right ear to the corner of his mouth.

You weren't supposed to stare at it. It was bad form. So I didn't.

"You're Nolan's boy, right?" His voice was quiet and smooth. Like butter.

Nolan. Jim Nolan. I was hoping to avoid that whole part of things.

It was a little bit of a standoff at the moment, between Dante and Jim. Jim controlled pretty much everything as far as vice was concerned in town, but Dante had been looking to make his move on him for a while. But that was none of my concern. I didn't work for Jim, I was just a friend. Kind of. It was complicated. "I don't work for him, I just know him."

"Saved his kid's life, from what I understand, back in the war."

"That's about the size of it."

Dante speared a small bite of his fish. "Too bad the kid died here."

That was the other part of it. Rumor was it had been Dante who had ordered the hit, originally meant for Jim, that got his son by mistake. But that was just a rumor on the street, not a story. Rumors were less reliable.

Dante took a small drink from his glass of red wine. He seemed to enjoy the taste of it in his mouth. He swished it back and forth, then swallowed. "Well, it's too bad you're not here from Jim. I thought maybe he sent you so he could just give everything to me."

"I don't think that's how Jim would work."

Dante actually smiled. "Neither do I." He raised a red napkin to his lips and cleaned himself. "So what's this about Liliana? It ought to be good, considering she's dead."

"She is. But some questions came up about the case. I was hired for the guy who was convicted of it."

"I was thinking about Liliana today. All the papers talking about the hanging tomorrow, you can't avoid it. Seems like the case is over, don't you think? "

"I thought it was too, until his mother came to visit me."

Dante looked up at me for the first time since I'd shown up. "What about his mother?"

"She came to see me this morning. Seems to think he's innocent." I looked at Dante, just trying to see if there was any kind of reaction. There wasn't. But he had stopped eating.

He nodded his chin toward me. "What do you think?"

I felt like being honest, although I always feel like being honest. It was a fault of mine. "It seems like he got railroaded. A nice easy guy to pin it on. Works as a waiter, completely out of his league, and he gets hit with the murder rap. I'm not saying he's an angel; he's a bit of an ass, to be honest. But I don't like innocent guys to die for something they didn't do. And besides, his mother got to me."

"What'd she say?"

"She didn't want to lose him."

Dante laughed a little under his breath. Then he got busy with his food again. "Too many mothers lose their sons. It's how the world works."

Dante hadn't brought his eyes back up to mine; he kept focusing on his food. I have a theory that if you want to know something, you ask. It's a pretty simple theory. Even if sometimes it might get you killed. "Did you do it?"

The three guys standing in back of Dante slammed their eyes to me pretty quickly, then started walking to me fast.

Dante raised a hand to calm them.

They stopped.

Dante looked back up at me. Another smile played across his mouth, then widened to what looked like joy. A regular miracle. "I like you, you know that?"

"I'm glad you approve." I actually was. It was better than dying.

"You got something about you. Maybe stupidity." Then he outright laughed.

"I've been told that."

"But as far as Liliana, even if I did do anything to her, I wouldn't tell you anyway."

"I didn't think you would. But sometimes people's actions speak more."

"And what do mine tell you?"

Honestly, he was too loose. Crime doesn't have much to do with the truth, but as far as he was talking there in front of me, he seemed straight. "That maybe you didn't do it."

"You're a good PI, then."

He pushed his plate of food away and, instantly, one of the three goons took it.

Apparently the boys were versatile.

Then Dante pulled a cigarette case from out of his jacket pocket and everything changed. Kind of.

The case was gold, smooth gold, and in the center of the face of it was an *M* etched in. And the *M* was surrounded by a circle.

Hmm... interesting.

I'd only gotten a flash of it before he opened the case, but after he had pulled a cigarette out and closed the case back up and set it on the red tabletop, there it was. The *M* was etched in a plain block style, and the circle around it was actually a circle — of intricate scrollwork.

Just like the lighter found next to Liliana.

Only it wasn't.

"You like it?" Dante motioned toward the case.

The scrollwork was more intricate than the lighter in the photo, but the *M* in the middle looked… similar. But not.

I was confused.

Not least of all because of how stupid I was. An *M* for Miles? Or an *M* for Manzione. How had the cops not even thought of that?

Right. Because they already had Miles.

I kept looking at the case. "It's… interesting."

"My mother gave it to me. Solid gold. A going away present." Then from his jacket he also pulled out a small gold lighter that matched the case and, yeah, it had the *M* and circle of intricate scrollwork around it.

The *M* and circle on the lighter matched the *M* and circle on the cigarette case. But neither matched exactly the lighter in the photo that was found next to Liliana when she died. But it was interesting how close it was.

Like clumsily interesting.

Like if you knew Dante and wanted to frame him, dropping a bad version of a very nice lighter at a crime scene might just get the job done.

If the cops were blind.

Or… if they were paid to be blind.

Dante looked up at me and puffed on his cigarette, smoke trailing over the table. "I hate when mothers lose sons. I've been to enough funerals. It's the worst part."

I wondered how many funerals Dante had caused himself. I never thought of him as the sentimental type.

But then he just sat there, with his cigarette and half-empty glass of wine. He didn't much move, staring forward to the other side of the empty booth. I wasn't sure what he was thinking of, or what was going through his mind.

Maybe mothers and funerals.

He didn't look up, but he did talk, to the other side of the booth. The empty side. "You look at Gold yet?"

"Honestly? I'm looking at your lighter. With the *M* on it."

Dante picked it up, turned it over in his hand, then brought up the *M* side again, right there in front of us, glinting in the low light of the restaurant, over a deep red table cloth. "He's a bastard, you know."

"Who?"

"Gold."

"I'm not doubting you, but why do you say it?"

Dante took another pull from his cigarette and let the smoke just trail out of his mouth and drift lazily up to toward the dark ceiling to join the rest of the smoke.

"That last night, we were all over at the Papaya Room."

"You, Liliana, Gold, and Daisy and James from the restaurant."

"And Daisy and James from the restaurant." Dante looked like he was remembering the scene, but there was a strange, detached quality to him.

"So what happened?"

Dante kept staring at the empty booth in front of him. "She was in a mood."

"Liliana?"

"Yeah, Liliana. Telling us all to basically go to hell."

"How'd that sit with you?"

Dante looked up at me, a little annoyed at the question I think. His scar caught the light. I wondered what happened to the other guy. "Didn't bother me a bit." He shifted back to looking at the empty seat in front of him and blew out another long stream of smoke.

Truth be told, it looked like it did bother him a bit what Liliana had said. About how she was kicking him out of the restaurant.

Her restaurant. But I decided not to mention a thing.

"She had enough for all of us, but she saved the best for Gold. He's on the wrong side of this Depression, did you know that?"

It made sense, I guessed. Maybe even the great Golden Pictures. "No, I didn't."

Dante got a faraway, happy look on his face. Like he was thinking of a dame. "He was hurting for dough. And Liliana? She was giving him trouble. Did you hear about the new contract?"

I played dumb. "What contract?"

Dante smiled. "The one I was helping Liliana renegotiate."

Okay. That was a surprise.

Then he laughed. "The one I was helping her rewrite."

This was getting even better.

"Do you know what he was back east?"

"Gold?"

"Yeah. I knew him back then. Before I moved here. We both ran in the same circles, so to speak." A small smile formed at the side of Dante's mouth. "He had to get out of town back then." Then a small smile broke into a large laugh. "He thought he was something back then. But he wasn't." Then the smile faded. "He tried to cross me, and I almost got him. But he had to run out of town because of something else."

This was getting a little far afield, and sounded like it was more of a grudge between these two than anything else. And Dante was adding a little to Gold's pain. "What about the contract?"

"She told Gold she was finished. Unless he signed the new contract. The old one was pretty bad and he pretty much took everything she made for him. She got some, but not what she was worth. So he wasn't happy about a new contract. Not at all."

"Okay, so he wasn't happy. He's the head of a movie studio."

Dante looked up at me. "And what's your point?"

"It's a movie studio. It's not like you and Jim. He's not going to go out and kill his top star."

He shook his head. "You know nothing, do you."

Then he sat back in the booth and crossed his leg. He looked like a lounging viper. He took another pull off his cigarette, the end turning the bright color of a setting sun, then he exhaled through the corner of his mouth. The side next to the scar. "Do you know why he left New York?"

"No."

"Well, you should look it up."

"Miles gets hanged tomorrow at midnight. I don't exactly have the time to be running down that little piece of information. If you can enlighten me, I'd be very much…" I was about to say obliged. Bad mistake. "I would appreciate it very much."

"Enough to tell Nolan to get out of town?"

"I told you already, I don't work for him. That's between the two of you. And I tend to be smart enough not to get between."

"Good for you."

"If you could tell me…" I decided to try something, "I'm sure Miles' mother would appreciate it."

Dante looked directly at me and, for the first time, I could see in his dark eyes that there was something maybe a little more deep than what I had heard on the street.

He crushed out his cigarette into the small, round glass ashtray with Little Pete's spelled out in the bottom of it. In red. "It was for murder. And he did it."

Then Dante picked up his napkin and dabbed the corner of his mouth, and out of nowhere the three goons behind me had me by the shoulders and gave me the bum's rush out of the place.

I was out and onto the sidewalk in front of the place in no time flat, the three of them walking back through the red door that I was just rushed out of.

The door closed slow behind them and I stood still there on the sidewalk, next to a relatively busy Broadway, cars and trucks motoring past on their way into and out of downtown.

The sun beat down and I felt the heat rise up from the sidewalk beneath me.

I looked back up Broadway toward downtown, and the white granite tower of City Hall rose up like a beacon. Telling me that yes, this is Los Angeles. Where mob bosses negotiated contracts for movie stars, and movie moguls might be committing murder.

Chapter 17

CARDON SAT IN A small office at the LA courthouse.

He didn't want to be looking at case files anywhere where Price and Black, or any of the other detectives, could see him.

It was just easier this way. No need for anyone to see one detective looking at the case file for someone else's case. He could have made up some lie that it related to a case he was currently working on, but who needed to lie?

The nice thing about case files was that there are always copies of them. At LAPD, at the prosecutor's office, and if it went to trial, there was always a copy at the courthouse located right near City Hall.

Convenient.

And that's where Cardon was. In a small, windowless room near the records office, looking at a file.

That was very, very thin.

There were photos of the crime scene — Liliana McGann lying on the floor of her restaurant, strangled with one of the long cloth napkins from her own place. Plus a photo of a lighter with an *M* and a kind of circle around it in scrollwork. But beyond that, there wasn't much else.

A few notes from only one interview that night, with Miles White, stating that he and Liliana had had a fight that night. She left, he got drunk, and he woke up when the police started shaking him.

And that was that.

No other interviews, no other nothing. It's like the case began, and ended, with Miles.

And that didn't make a whole lot of sense. Price and Black had looked at no other person, didn't question anyone else she was with that night, nothing. Except one small note that Liliana's co-owners in the restaurant had positively identified the lighter as having belonged to Miles.

And that note came from two days after the murder.

Convenient.

That was the only word that kept running around inside Cardon's brain as he looked at basically nothing spread out in front of him.

Convenient.

Chapter 18

I WALKED IN AND Charlie was finally in the office. Mainly because Bella was gone.

She had him downstairs in a large storage area I rented in addition to the offices. Filing. Or rather, getting all of it a bit more organized from when I first started the business.

She'd probably have him down there for five years. I felt sorry for the kid. He was starting to look pasty. "Where's Bella?"

"At the lawyer's. Mrs. White called over there to give permission."

"Good."

Charlie looked at me. "Is there anything I can do, Mr. Devin? I want to help."

He was a good kid.

He sat there at a small folding Coca-Cola card table I bought for two dollars. I had felt sorry for him being in the basement all the time filing, so I picked up the card table to at least give him a place of his own, so to speak, up here with actual people. I don't know what he did, though, that was for Bella to take care of.

Charlie'd shown up one day looking for a job after his old man had thrown him out of the house. In the middle of the

Depression. He hadn't eaten or slept in three days. I gave him a job and got him a place to stay.

Now I guessed he was my responsibility.

One, to be honest, I didn't mind. He was a good kid. "No, Charlie. Whatever you're doing for Bella is great. I appreciate it."

"But—"

The door to the office opened and Bella walked in.

She was a little startled to see me, then headed straight for her desk.

I looked at the manila file in her hand. "Is that it?"

Bella handed it to me.

It was thin. "And that's it?"

"That's all I got." She didn't look happy.

I was less happy. This couldn't be all of it. "Was it the girl or Streck who gave it to you?"

"The girl. And her name is June. And you know that." Bella was definitely cranky.

"Fine, June. And that's all she gave you?"

Bella set her purse on the floor next to her. She thought for a few seconds, then looked up at me. "I'm beginning to think you were right. The way she handed it over—"

"June?"

"Yes, June. The way she looked at me, or didn't look at me, like she was avoiding me, made me think that there was more that should have been in it. But she had—"

"Well, can't you go back and get it from her?"

"Would you stop interrupting me?"

Definitely cranky. "Whatever it was, it came from Streck. He's the one not giving it all. And no, I can't go back and ask her for the rest of it. If it even exists. You saw her, Devin, and you saw the way he treated her. The girl is lucky she has a job. She has a kid, did you know that?"

I didn't.

"And there was no way that I was going to beat her up like Streck did, just to get whatever else there was. He called her worthless. When I got there."

That I didn't like, and I made a mental note to go back and visit the jackass. After we got finished with whatever happened with Miles.

Miles.

I looked through the file, and there was basically nothing. Except the picture of the lighter, which I already had, and a few notes. Nothing much else. Nothing that looked like Horace P. Streck had investigated anything that Miles had told him about.

It was like he had wanted him guilty.

Of course. There was a lot stinking about this case.

"And while you're working on that, do you have any ideas on how you're going to finish the Crouse case?"

Bella stared at me and I didn't answer.

"Okay, then how about the Hanson case. Or the Kirkman case? Anything there?"

"Look, Bella, you know I have to work on this one now."

"I'm telling you, John, let's split the work. I can help."

"Are you an investigator?"

And she stopped. Talking. And she looked at me with something in those brown eyes that I didn't particularly like.

As in something she wasn't telling me. "What?"

Then she got hard. And gave me a look trying to be innocent, but held the punch of steel. "What do you mean, what?"

"I mean what's going on? You're quiet."

Bella swallowed, then leaned back in her chair, arms crossed in front of her. Her red lipstick looked even more red than usual. Like it was blood. "I've applied for a detective's license."

"A what?!"

"A detective's license." She came right back at me, ready for a fight. "Do you have a problem with that?"

Well, Bella looked like she had a problem with it. A big one, and I didn't even know what was going on.

I looked over at Charlie and his jaw was wide open, and not like it was going to be closing any time soon.

I checked my own jaw. It was still shut. Good. But I had to think.

She smiled. "There's nothing to think about."

Again with the mind reading. "Why?"

Bella let out a noise halfway between a grunt and the disgusted sound of a parent not believing how stupid their child could be. Then she opened up her desk drawer and dropped a set of manila file folders about ten inches thick on top of her desk. "Because of these, you thick-headed beast."

Now nobody had ever called me a beast. Because I wasn't. I didn't think I was. "Wh... wh..."

Bella's eyes got tight. "You need help and you can't even begin to let anyone do it. So I figured I had better do something about it."

"But..."

"But what? Are you going to tell me I can't? Because I already have."

"You got it already?"

"No. Within the next month. They have the application, but I should have it within the next month."

I looked at Charlie and somehow his surprise had faded into... admiration.

"You don't have to let me use it if you don't want, but you'd be an idiot if you didn't. And here." Bella handed me a piece of paper with a phone number on it.

"What's that?"

"The number for a judge."

"Why would I want a judge?"

"Because, if you want to stop a certain execution tomorrow night, you need to get a judge to call up to the Meck and let them know he's issuing a stay of execution. That's the only way they'll stop it. And most likely, you'll need someone from LAPD to convince the judge."

I hadn't even thought of that. Any of that. And she had.

Bella sat back in her chair with a mix of anger, fear, and downright cussed-stubbornness.

And honest to God, I was impressed. I held up the paper she had handed to me. "Where'd you get this?"

She didn't answer for a bit. I suppose to calm down a bit. "I have a friend over at the LA courthouse. She told me what we would need. That's the number for a judge. She said he'd actually done it twice before so he knows what he's doing."

"What's his name?"

"Judge Stanley."

Judge Stanley. I'd been in front of him before. A few too many times, as a matter of fact… for less than legal activities. What can I say, I went all out for my clients. "Is there anyone else?"

Bella looked at me, like I was looking a gift horse in the mouth. "Do you want me to find another? I can call her back. If you don't mind me actually *helping* you on something."

She was probably about to haul off and hit me. Charlie, to his credit, got his face buried back in whatever paperwork he was doing on his card table. For his sake, I hoped it was Bella's filing.

"I know, but…" I looked at Bella sitting there, and she really was good. And smarter than me sometimes. Hell, most times. "There's one other guy I want to check. A judge that I kind of know."

A judge I at least had never been in front of.

And I hoped, may think he owed me something.

Then the phone rang.

Bella picked it up and, after a few back-and-forths along with a raised eyebrow, she hung up the phone and looked at me. "Aren't you lucky."

"What?" I wondered if Streck had reconsidered on any extra evidence he may have.

"It was Louis Gold's office. He wants you to come over."

"Me? When?"

"Now."

"Now?"

"Don't be a parrot. Yes, now."

Okay, there was a lot going on, and my head was more than

full. "A detective's license…"

"Yes."

The fight had gone out of Bella and to be honest, it was out of me, too. I didn't know what to think.

I held up the note with the phone number on it. "Thanks for this."

Bella didn't say anything.

But I did. "And for thinking."

She snorted. "Someone had to."

I nodded. Then got up to leave.

"Wait." Bella reached for another piece of paper and handed it to me. "Your judge is going to need this."

I looked at the paper. It had another phone number on it. This one long distance. "What is it?"

"The number to the Meck, to the gallows room." Bella smiled like she completely had me. And she did. "Your judge is going to need it."

Yep. That he would.

I gave her back a smile myself. "Thank you." And I hoped she knew that I meant it.

Then I got myself out of there because my brain was full.

And I had to get it back on the case, because that was the only way that Miles was going to make it through tomorrow night.

At least I hoped he did. Because there was a little old lady I definitely didn't want to disappoint.

By losing her son.

Her only family.

And that hit home hard.

Because I knew what it was like not to have one. And for her, for that little old lady — I was definitely not going to let that happen.

Chapter 19

I HAD BEEN TO a number of studios before, but never to Golden.

Golden Pictures was the biggest and glitziest studio in Hollywood. Located right in the middle of Hollywood, it took up a full square mile.

I entered off Melrose Avenue through the Melrose Gate. It was actually one great gate with two arches; one in, and the other out.

The gate itself looked like a million bucks. It was large, standing thirty feet tall, and covered in the light, pinkish-white stucco that seemed to cover everything in Southern California. Two huge black wrought iron gates were there to close everything off but they were swung wide and welcoming. Opening to a PI who had no business being in a place like this.

The gate itself was covered in fancy scrollwork like something lifted off a Spanish building the scrollwork covered in gold, as was the giant script *G* in the middle of a circle of... golden scrollwork. Hmm... and it reminded me of the *M* and scrollwork on the face of the lighter that Miles never saw in his life.

Interesting, and for a fleeting second I wondered if Louis

Gold had a middle name that began with an *M*.

I pulled forward to the small guard shack in front of me, and a nice young guard in a spiffy new dark blue uniform, complete with a golden *G* with golden scrollwork circle on the chest, came out to ask me my business.

I gave him my name and that must have done something because he let me on the lot. After he told me where to go.

And he was pleasant about it. Imagine that.

As I drove in I could see that my gunmetal blue Model A was outclassed in this joint. I headed forward to where I was told, to a parking area dead center of the lot.

There were Cadillacs, Bugattis, Packards, and a few Rolls-Royces.

I was a kid originally from Michigan and if you were from Michigan, you knew cars. Even the ones you dreamed of. And that lot in the middle of Golden Pictures was a parking lot full of dreams.

I pulled my Model A up between a red Isotta Fraschini and a bright blue Cord and didn't allow myself to look at their low, smooth, curved lines or at the paint that looked like it had been laid on with at least a hundred layers of hand-painted perfection. I didn't look.

But I could feel them there. Resting charged and waiting to fly on either side of me. So I got myself the hell away from them as fast as I could.

They were like dames — no need being tempted by something you couldn't have.

Most of the buildings around the parking area were the large, rectangular types that looked like airplane hangars. With their slightly curved tops, they were the sound stages where all the movies were shot. Although here at Golden Pictures they seemed to be a little larger and a little more beautiful than the sound stages at the other lots I had been on. All of them were painted the same pinkish-white of the main front gate, as was every building that I could see as a matter of fact.

Each of the sound stages had a big number painted on its

edge. 31 lay in front of me, 24 over to my right, with 7 and 8 over to my left.

A lot of people walked around as I got out of the parking area and onto the lot proper. Life, that's what it looked like. A living, breathing place with a lot of people who looked like they had someplace to go. And the one thing that I did like was I saw a lot of common people. In among the suits and dresses that walked back and forth, there were workers dressed in everything from coveralls to uniforms, dungarees to blue work shirts. A nice mix.

And I had to admit, there was a certain peace here at the studio.

Everything was clean and orderly, everything looked like it had been painted yesterday. And there were even perfectly clipped bushes sprouting around and along the walkways to make the place look downright nice.

The guard at the gate had told me to take Avenue L to the corner of 7th Street. Wherever that was.

It was only Louis Gold waiting for me, so I figured I would take a stroll first. I'd never been to Golden Pictures before and I thought what the heck, while I was here, take a look around.

Because I was probably never coming back.

The one thing people never thought of was that this was just an industry like everything else. Like Mr. Ford's cars. Turning one out after another, and hope that something hit.

Maybe it was more like panning for gold, I guess that was better. Although here it's not like you have a pan — you have an entire square mile, filled with people, running around doing your bidding. And coming up with movies that, for the most part, have happily-ever-after endings, and you hope at least one, or a few, ended up as a large chunk of gold.

It seemed like Liliana McGann was as close to a chunk of gold as you could get in this business. And as much as I'd heard from everyone so far, it was in all their interests to keep her safe — and definitely not kill her.

A lot of people lived off of her, I thought, and it seemed no one would want her dead. But someone did.

Looking around at the large buildings as I walked, and all the people, I knew somebody was making gold around here and most likely, it was King Louis. I wondered if that was his real last name.

Now if you listen to the fan magazines, Louis Gold came out here in search of gold — get it? But there was a darker side, too.

I had already heard there were stories that he had to get out of New York after a run-in with a few people. I don't know who those people were, but after what Dante had said, my imagination did the guessing.

Straight from the streets of New York, Louis Gold was supposed to be a piece of work. Got himself successful by the bootstraps. Then there were other stories where he didn't care who got in his way.

As I looked around the studio, everything was clean, everything was nice, and everybody pretty much had a smile as they passed me. I suppose it also helped having a job during the Depression. You'd smile at everything if you kept getting paid each day.

I found 7th Street and made a left. It was kind of interesting, the street names, named after New York. But they were actually pretty narrow. About the size of two car-widths across if they were even that. I suppose that made sense, though, with all the big buildings around here, you had to fit them in somewhere. And if you needed another sound stage, you made the road smaller. You used everything you had.

7th was lined with the tall, huge sound stages running down a good long ways. At each one, a ramp headed up to a doorway about ten feet off the street. My guess was to move the lights and anything else that needed to go in and out.

Ahead at sound stage 14, a guy in a pirate costume stood at the top of one of the ramps, smoking a cigarette. Except his costume was more like something from a burlesque show, complete with a bright blue feather shot out of the middle of his enormous hat, a bright blue jacket like something from 1700s England, and bright red pants, large as something on a clown. He looked at me and then smiled.

Then he laughed and shrugged his shoulders.

I almost felt sorry for the guy, dressed up like that, but then right in that instant I got the whole craziness of this place.

I smiled back at him and nodded. He nodded back, took another draw off his cigarette, and walked back in through the door that shut behind him. Off to make dreams, I guessed.

Somebody's dreams anyway.

And then I saw it ahead: the Louis Gold Building.

Home of the king.

Chapter 20

AS BUILDINGS GO, IT wasn't opulent, it wasn't huge, and it wasn't tall. But you definitely got the feeling of power from the place.

A rather large building, maybe a hundred feet across, it rose three stories up in the same Spanish style as the main entry gate of the studio, but here it had an understated power to it. You knew there was something special here.

The entrance was a large section that projected out from the building and into the street in front, with large blocks of windows on the second and third floors that wrapped around the section and looked out onto everything below. I imagined Louis up in one of those areas, looking out over the studio that he had built. It's where I would have put myself.

A king, overlooking his land.

I walked up the five concrete steps of the entrance and inside.

Into plainness.

A regular building inside with no receptionist, but I suppose that was about correct. Anyone who worked on this lot knew where they needed to go and didn't need anyone to tell them. The guard told me to go up to the third floor, but gave me no idea of which office to go to exactly.

I saw the stairs to my right and started to walk up.

It was all very plain, but every detail seemed to yell out money, sophistication, and power. The stair steps were a spotless black with small, pinkish-white specks twirling through them, the marble paneled walls seeming to take those same pinkish-white specks and fill themselves with them. It was simple, but the more I rose, the more I could tell that this wall must have cost a fortune.

I wondered just how many people it took to place these marble panels and tiles perfectly together so that it looked like all of it was a stairway full of stars. I laughed and, indeed, stars it was, all over the walls. And I wondered how many times Liliana had walked up these very steps. How much of it she had paid for with her movies.

I finally made it to the third floor and saw why I didn't need a room number. The stairs emptied into a large open area made of the same black marble on the floor and the lighter marble on the walls, and one single desk in the middle of it.

Chairs lined the outer walls, with only one set of doors leading anywhere else. A double set, actually, as tall as the fifteen-foot ceiling in the room. The doors had black padding on them that looked like leather, with gold buttons punched in so it looked like a sofa seat. Then I saw the buttons themselves, engraved with the golden *G* logo of the studio. A man marking his territory.

I went to the center desk and a nice older woman sat there with white hair and a white blouse. "May I help you?"

She was clean and efficient, and knew that I didn't belong here. She wasn't bad about it, but I could tell from her look: I definitely didn't belong here.

"I'm John Devin, here to see Mr. Gold."

As she got on the phone to call someone, I looked around the office.

In the corners, small groups of people huddled. One set of three people sat with what looked like a bunch of battered pieces of paper between them. The pages were dog-eared and abused, and all stuck together. Most likely a script.

One guy of the group looked harried and almost as beaten-up as the script. Probably the writer. Another guy, one with an honest to God brown tam on his head and a riding crop in his hand, was probably the director. I almost laughed out loud. I thought they only looked that way in the pictures. He'd obviously seen too many of them and bought the look hook, line, and sinker.

In the other corners and along the wall were other groups of people waiting to go in to see the king. Most of them didn't look comfortable, and every one of them looked like they wanted to be somewhere else.

"Mr. Gold will see you now." The older woman gestured over to the two large doors, just as a nice looking woman walked out of them.

And I'll be damned… it was Tracy Sinclaire. An actress in a couple of pictures I'd actually seen. She wasn't bad looking in real life. Check that, she was stunning in real life. Her long chestnut hair hung loose over her short, light pink silk dress that looked like it had just walked in off a summer field of flowers.

Her eyes flicked across the room as she headed to the stairs and fell on me.

They were blue. I could see that much anyway, and she didn't leave them off me as she made it to the stairs and disappeared down, I swear, a small smile on her face as she did.

Hmm…

"Mr. Devin…"

I turned around to the older woman at the desk. She had a stern look on her face that shot out from a set of glasses she must have put on when I wasn't looking. To be accurate, when I was looking at Miss Sinclaire. With the new glasses in place, the old woman looked like a real den mother. As in a bear.

I guess I needed to go.

And I did.

To the great double doors that Miss Sinclaire had just exited.

On the other side of the great black doors was another office, and beyond that, another set of doors. Only those doors were made of gold. Honest to God, complete gold. Not the color and not the paint, but the real shiny stuff, and it had that deep, almost rose golden color of the 24K stuff, and in the middle of it was engraved the famous *G*, inside the circling scrollwork.

Any ideas of anyone but Louis Gold being beyond those doors was just plain stupid. I had reached the inner sanctum. The lair of the king.

This second reception area was closed, hushed, and silent in there as the black doors closed behind me. I didn't know if they did it automatically or servants had shut them behind me.

There were only three people in this outer office and I was one of them. Another was an accountant-looking guy in round glasses holding a black attaché case, and the third was a blonde-haired goddess sitting behind the only desk. I was waiting for angels to sing. Then she did.

"Hello, Mr. Devin, so good of you to come."

She was speaking to me. Amazing. And it sounded like she was whispering it just to me. If this was a reception area, I was in the reception room to Heaven.

"Mr. Gold will be with you in just a moment."

Her lipstick was a soft red, her skin was light and white, her beautiful soft dress a deep green the color of trees back home in Michigan. In spring. When all was fresh.

I realized I was staring, smirked a little bit, and then headed to a chair in the corner. As far away from her as I could get.

I was afraid the den mother from outside might have followed me.

I didn't even get the chance to set myself down when the soft opening of a very large door sounded from behind me.

"Devin."

I turned. Max.

His body shot toward me like an arrow. It amazed me how much energy the guy had. And he still had that smile. "I appreciate your coming. Mr. Gold can be pretty insistent when he wants things."

"And how often does he get what he wants?"

Max just smiled.

"Got it."

Max motioned me toward the golden door and I walked in to Louis Gold's office.

And it was as big as a house.

Chapter 21

LOUIS GOLD'S OFFICE WAS bright. It shined and gleamed from every corner, and in every crease.

The carpet was a deep gold and felt thick as a cloud. Three main seating areas were scattered around the place, with what looked like a complete bar tucked in the corner to the left. Prohibition did not touch this man.

And there were flowers. Today must have been white day. There were white roses — countless white roses — orchids, tulips, and apple blossoms tinged in pink. And groups and bunches of white calla lilies. My favorite, actually.

The man had taste. Or whoever decorated his office did.

Five movie posters sat framed in gold around the walls, three of them with Liliana front and center. Then there were the photos, hung from the walls and clustered and stuffed on every available flat surface. One of the flat surfaces included a white grand piano just in front of me, in the middle of the place.

A couple of small trees sat potted in the corners, and a commanding crystal chandelier hung over a small dining table to the side that I would assume... was where the man went in case he got hungry.

In back of me and to the left, against the wall, were two world-class goons. Strong-arm types, who looked like they made their living inside a boxing ring. Smashed noses and scarred faces, one was short and hard, the other tall and mean. And both had completely bald heads. What was it with jerks in bald heads lately? Between these two guys and Dee and Dumb, I was up to my eyes in them.

To ease my eyes, I looked back at the rest of King Louis' lair. And to his desk.

It was to my right and it was massive. The size of three of my desks. It was modern, with sharp edges, and was made of glass and about three different kinds of light-colored wood from somewhere far away. Places I was sure I had never been. A regular piece of sculpture.

And sitting behind it, and just in front of what looked like a row of at least ten Academy Awards on a credenza and a large window beyond that, was the man himself. Louis Gold.

Gangster, moviemaker, king of this world that he owned.

Louis got up with what almost passed as a smile and walked directly at me. Like a torpedo seeking a big fat boat.

He looked about the same as I'd seen in the newspapers. A great slab of a man. He stood my equal at six feet, but he had a combination of flab around the midsection and around his face, heading up to his partially bald head. Yet underneath all of that, you could tell that he was hard as a rock.

And willing to use it.

"Mr. Devin." The great Louis stretched his hand out toward me and looked at the floor as he did.

I wasn't sure if it was because he didn't care who I was, or didn't want to trip in his own office. I took the offered hand and it was a strong grip. Very strong.

And I looked at him. And he finally did look at me. His eyes were a deep brown, like they were pulled from the loam of a deep, deep canyon. And it was interesting, there was a certain something that came off the man. Confidence, I suppose you could say.

I'd seen it in some generals that I had talked with during the war. They knew that their every command would be followed. They knew that they made decisions that would kill men and liberate countries. And everyone knew they were full of themselves. "Care for a drink?"

Over Louis' desk was the set of windows that looked out over his studio, over his kingdom. I could see straight up 7th Street. "Sure." I needed something to keep me awake. And besides, my guess was he had the good stuff. I didn't get enough of that.

Max was already on the way over to the bar.

That's when I saw a medium-sized guy sitting alone on the end of a large black sofa against the wall. A glass coffee table sat in front of him with a low arrangement of white roses on top of it. The guy had on a black suit, like an undertaker. That's probably why I missed him on the black sofa.

And he wasn't an accountant.

You could tell by the look. He had been in the war. It took a Marine to recognize… well, he wasn't a Marine, that I could tell, but he was some kind of former soldier. And he kept quiet about it.

"I'd like you meet Stan." Gold was already on the way over to the black sofa. "He's my head of security."

Stan was in his mid-forties somewhere, with a hard lean jaw, lighter than normal lips, and a face that looked like it never much got out in the Southern California sun. As in, like an undertaker. Like his suit. But there was a hardness under it all that almost matched Louis'. Make that he matched it, but where Louis' was the hardness of a battering ram, Stan's was the hardness of a sharp edge of granite.

Louis directed me to a single, black leather chair opposite the sofa. Stan didn't get up as I sat and didn't offer me his hand. But he did offer me his eyes. Staring at me as I sat. Getting a measure of me.

It didn't bother me one bit.

I'd met a lot of guys who'd try to intimidate you just for sport.

Intimidation didn't work on me. And as a matter of fact, it made me feisty.

Max handed me a drink. "Here you go."

I took the glass from Max and noticed I was the only one with one. Well, I wasn't going to let that get in my way. I took a nice big sip of the golden booze inside. It was scotch. I was right. The good stuff.

Gold sat in the middle of the couch, and reached into a large dish on the coffee table in front of him, grabbed a handful of peanuts, salted they looked like, and chucked the entire mess into his mouth. "So what you doing about this Liliana McGann case?"

At least that's what I thought he said.

I couldn't quite make it out clearly, as bits of gnashed peanut dropped and shot out of his mouth.

I hated people who talked with their mouths full. "Just asking some questions."

"What have you found so far?" Louis dove his fist back into the dish and jammed some more of the things into his face.

I was already feeling thirsty myself just watching it all, so I took another long sip of his good scotch. "Not a lot, but I'll come back with a report anytime you like." I tipped the glass to Louis. "Especially if I can have another drink like this."

Gold didn't laugh.

Max offered to help a little bit. I guess that's what PR guys do. "Mr. Gold is curious, only because he has the new Liliana McGann picture opening tomorrow. And you're welcome to come if you'd like."

I wasn't sure about the premier, but as far as the picture, that was another thing that I didn't understand from Max's visit to my office. I wasn't sure how things worked here in Hollywood, but out in the real world, once someone was dead, they didn't do much work after. "A picture with Miss McGann?"

Gold kept his mouth shut. I guess because he had people to do the talking for him.

So Max jumped in. Again. "Yes, like I mentioned before,

Liliana's last picture. We had most of it shot before she… died."

"Was murdered." I pointed out. Because I was feisty.

"Yes, murdered." Max had the decency to take a moment at least. I'm not sure that Louis would have. "It's taken a year to finish it, but it's actually a great picture. Might even get one of those." Max pointed over at the row of Academy Awards. I hadn't noticed before, but they looked like ducks lined up at a shooting gallery.

"I'm a kind of curious guy, so I'm wondering how she's releasing a picture when she's been dead for a year."

"*I* release the picture… Mr. Devin, is it?"

He knew my name.

"The actors only star in them. And I could put another actor in any of them just as easy as pie." Then Louis smiled. "It's magic here." I knew he was trying to mean the studio, but the way he said it, sitting there in the middle of that black couch, it was as if he had pulled the entire studio inside of him. Into that great battering ram of a body sitting opposite me. "And we can do anything we want."

Then he rammed his fist back down into the dish of salted peanuts, a few peanuts dropping to the coffee table in small little glass plinks.

Then Louis waved his fist in the air, happy and smiling like a kid who'd gotten everything he ever wanted. "If I want to make a picture with Liliana — I make a picture with Liliana. It's that easy." Then he shoved the nuts into his face and started to chew with his mouth open.

I really hated that.

Max jumped in. "We had most of it shot, and then we—"

Louis shut Max up with a stare. I got the impression that he didn't like to be interrupted.

I kinda felt sorry for Max. From the look that Louis gave him, I wasn't sure there would be much of him left after I left. Maybe Louis'd hit him with one of those Academy Awards. It would be a perfect blunt object.

"Like I was saying," Gold cut into the silence, "We can do

anything we want. Max was right, we had most of it in the can when she went and got herself killed. We had to rewrite a few things, put a couple a stand-ins in, but this is the movies so like I said — it's magic — so we made the picture. Now I've got a lot of money in this thing, Mr. Devin. And I don't want to see anything happen to my investment. And you asking questions around only brings up the kind of publicity that I don't want for this picture."

I looked at Gold and took another sip of his expensive booze. "Well, I don't mind asking the questions when a man's neck is on the line."

Gold got up and he wasn't happy. "Do you mean to tell me that a full police investigation, a full trial, and a jury finding him guilty — that there was any kind of problem in there?"

He was a tall boy to be standing over you, even if it was over a coffee table between us. "I don't know. That's why I'm looking."

Gold sat back down, disturbed. Maybe trying to get back on my level. Maybe trying to talk man to man instead of king to peon. "The guy is going to be executed tomorrow, am I right?"

I nodded. "That's about the gist of it."

"Well, it seems like it's all done but the noose." He looked at me, getting confidential, getting buddy-buddy. "What is it, money? Because if it's money, I think I can talk to Stan here and…" Louis looked at Stan for the first time. "We got things he can do around here, right?"

"Right." It was the first time Stan had spoken the entire time. His voice was cool as hard granite.

Gold was rolling now, still buddy-buddy. "My guess is, Stan here could keep you busy for a year."

"Sure." The second thing Stan said the entire time.

"Not a bad thing in the middle of a Depression, am I right?" Gold had solved everything, right there on his couch. I could see how he operated now. Brilliant ideas, and others take care of it. He didn't get his own hands dirty. "Chasing around on some case that everybody has given up on, and that the guy has been convicted of already, seems like a stupid use of time to me."

"Not to Miles White."

Louis just kept going. "And I know about time, let me tell you, Mr. Devin. I learned about time a long time ago. We don't get enough of it in the day. And it wastes away like sand. Flows like a river. And the thing about a river is it gets moving and it moves fast, and it even destroys things. Now, I think, if it was me, I would know a good thing when I saw it. What do you say?"

Despite the implied threat toward the end there, what was I supposed to say? I know one thing I could honestly say, I liked his booze.

But I also liked the fact that he talked a lot. It was telling me a lot of things. Obviously he didn't want me on the case, that was a given. But I was curious. "Why don't you want me asking around about this?"

Louis' face went hard. Even harder than what it was before. And if he hated people interrupting him, he really must hate them questioning him. But he held it in.

I had to give him credit for that.

He rose again off the black couch. "Let's take a walk."

Chapter 22

GOLD WALKED ME OUT himself, his arm around me, as Max and Stan walked behind us down Avenue L.

As we walked, the entire way through the spotless streets of the studio, people kept looking at him and saying "Hello, Mr. Gold," and "Good afternoon, Mr. Gold," until it got a little repetitive.

Actually it got a lot annoying.

Because each time they said it, they said it with a slight bow of their head and the quickening of a step. As if they wanted to get the hell away from the man as soon as they could. Hoping they wouldn't be swatted to the side, smashed against the side of a sound stage or into one of the fine and decorative bushes that lined the pristine walkways.

Louis walked like he knew where he was going and me sure as hell not. None of it looked familiar until we broke out into a gap between buildings and I could see the large parking area where my car was laid out in front of us.

Finally the end of the line, the end of the walk. Gold kept his hand around my shoulder like we were best of friends, or like the old reminder to keep your enemies closer. I knew I definitely wasn't his friend.

"I like to say you can judge a man by his shoes," Louis said as he glanced down at mine.

Mine were good, old-fashioned, sturdy brown brogues. A little worse for wear in places, but they got me places.

Louis' looked like they were made out of very expensive, very soft leather. Black they were, and so bright they looked like they had been shined by every person we had passed on the way here. Maybe everyone on the lot. They were that bright.

And they were tiny.

Smaller than I would have expected for a very big man.

"Think about what we talked about, and come to the right decision, Devin. I know you're smart."

He said that last as if it was a threat.

"I will. *Sir.*"

I threw in that last as a nice *stick you*. I think it stuck.

Because the great Louis Gold turned and left without saying good-bye.

As I watched his backside walk away, protected by Max to the left and the silent Stan to the right, I looked with a laugh as I saw people scurry to get out of his way.

Funny, I didn't think of Miles once while I was in there. Well, I did, but not like I had to clear him. Because now it seemed that Mr. Gold was just the kind of guy to have done what got done to Miss Liliana McGann. And Miles was just a convenient scapegoat.

But I wasn't sure.

And I would need to be.

If I was to convince a certain judge, who was just about to see me. And he didn't even know it.

Chapter 23

I GOT TO THE LA court building downtown a little later, and the judge's chambers were up on the third floor.

I walked into Judge Harry James' office, and an old gray-haired guy sat at the secretary's desk. He had to be in his mid-seventies, was thin, and his buttons were all buttoned, his tie was tied, and every hair seemed to be in place. Perfectly.

The exact opposite of me. "I was wondering if the judge was in?"

The old man looked at me with his mouth somewhere between a smile and a sneer, looking down at my rumpled pants, my wrinkled shirt, and a face that looked like it had been run through a ringer.

I smiled at him.

Probably a bad mistake.

"The judge is in a meeting right now," and the guy went back to looking at whatever file he had on his desk. I don't even think he was reading it.

I was just tired enough, and just delirious enough — or maybe I just didn't care — so I walked straight over to the judge's door and walked in.

I heard the old man in back of me protest loudly before I shut the door in his face.

And there Judge James sat, behind his desk, looking very, very angry.

As judges go, he looked exactly like a judge. His hair was gray. His well-trimmed mustache was gray. And his tie was tied perfectly and was dark gray. All in all, I wondered if his brother was the one I had met out front.

The judge, from the look in his eyes, wasn't used to people walking in on him.

"Judge James, I'm sorry to barge in on you, but—"

"You have two seconds to get out of my office." And he meant it.

I heard Gramps outside, banging on the door to get in. It's amazing: when you're half out of your mind, you can still remember to lock the door behind you. I guess it comes from old training.

But I had nothing to lose. "I'm sorry to do this, judge, but you're the only judge I know. I'm John Devin and I'm looking at the Miles White case. The guy who's about to be executed tomorrow."

The judge got up from behind his desk, reached into a desk drawer, and pulled out a gun and pointed it at me.

That, I didn't expect.

"I would suggest you unlock the door and get yourself out of here before I shoot you."

I looked at the hole in the front of the gun and guessed it was a .32. Plenty of bullet to kill me. Although from the look of him, I didn't think the judge would do it. Of course, that could just be the delirium. "Two things about you, Judge: I know you're honest, and you like to drink down at Toots'. So we got those two things going for us."

The judge hesitated for a second, and I saw him searching through his mind until yes, he finally recognized me. "You're the one who drinks for free there, right?"

I nodded at him. "Yeah, I did something for Toots one night."

"I know, I was there."

And that's what I had counted on.

That night, a few years back, I'd broken up a robbery that was happening at Toots'. And ever since, Toots would never let me pay for a drink. And kept a bottle of Jameson whiskey there just for me. A very rare thing in a Prohibition full of bathtub gin and rotgut whiskey.

I heard a key in the lock behind me and the door opened. Then in walked three court officers, followed by Gramps.

"It's all right," the judge said. "George, it's all right. Mr. Devin and I have a meeting."

I looked back at Gramps and decided not to rub salt in a wound, so I didn't smile at him.

Gramps and the officers left, closing the office door lightly behind them.

The judge, still holding the gun in his hand, looked down at it absent-mindedly. "I never pulled that out before."

I smiled. "Well, I have that effect on a lot of people."

The judge put the gun back into his desk drawer and sat down, heavily. He looked like he was shaken. I guess judges don't get much of a workout. At least when it comes to guns, people barging in, and people pushing into their lives.

Must be nice, I thought. I'd like a little bit of that life.

"So, what can I do for you, Mr. Devin?"

I had hoped it would go just this way. Well, not the part with the gun, or Gramps breaking in, but with the judge. See, he was at Toots' pretty much every night for the past three years. He mostly sat in a booth at the end of the place, which was where he had been the night Toots' was robbed. And I saved everyone in there from being robbed or having to answer to the cops.

I heard a rumor he'd started hanging out there regularly after his wife died. He never drank too much or anything. Usually just a beer or two. My guess was he was like me. It was a place to go that wasn't your empty apartment at night. Or in his case, maybe a large empty house in Hancock Park.

I didn't like people. But as much as I hated to admit it, I also didn't particularly like being alone.

So Toots' worked. Maybe for a lot of us.

I started. "The mother of Miles White came to me in my office this morning. And just looking at it today, there are a lot of problems with the case."

"Such as?"

I took a deep breath; this would take a while. "How about we start with a couple of police detectives who didn't look at anything past an engraved lighter. A lighter that Miles said he never knew of, never had, never saw before, and he doesn't smoke."

"I'm not going to retry the case right here, Mr. Devin. If there's new evidence, let me know. Otherwise there is nothing I can do."

"Well, I'm hoping to have some."

"When? Because he's being executed tonight, if I remember correctly?"

"You do. At midnight. The only thing I'm asking is… I hear the only way to stop this execution is through a stay of execution."

"That is correct. And you want me to issue that — because of something you did at a speakeasy that saved a number of people, including me, a number of years ago?"

"No. Because I think he's innocent. And was railroaded."

Judge James didn't say anything.

"And because I think you're honest. Maybe one of the only honest judges in LA."

"I will not have you, Mr. Devin, come in here to talk about the courts—"

"Because you know I'm right."

He didn't say anything.

I looked around his office for the first time since I'd entered.

There were more books than I'd seen in a library. But these were different. They were all volumes in a set. And taken together, they all looked like walls of knowledge. Sitting right there in front of me.

"Mr. Devin—"

"Just Devin."

"Devin… I don't know what I can do for you. You can't simply walk up to me and tell me someone is innocent."

"I'll find the evidence."

"And I cannot listen to you."

"I know. You have to hear it from a cop. What if I get one to tell you?"

"This is all the first I've heard of it, I can't possibly—"

"All I ask is that you give me a chance. I have someone on the LAPD helping me."

He brightened a bit. "You do?"

Well, I hoped I did. "Yes."

The judge sat at his desk, considering.

"Depending on what I… we, find, he'll be contacting you."

"Who is it?"

"Detective Henry Cardon."

"Yes. A good man."

He was. "We'll hope to have something for you by tomorrow."

"You had better."

"But if we don't, will you be at Toots' tomorrow night?"

He looked like he didn't want to answer. It was one thing to see him there night after night, but another for a sitting judge to admit that he actually frequented a speakeasy. Even if everyone in the city did.

He nodded.

I walked over to him and offered him my hand. "That's all I ask."

The judge took it and shook.

"And if I'm a little late, please stay. I'll have Toots take care of you."

"I don't need anyone to take care of me."

"I know. But… you'll be doing a good thing. You'll be there?"

He nodded again.

I reached into my jacket and pulled out a white piece of paper and handed it to him.

He took it. "What is this?"

"The number to the Meck. Directly into the room."

He looked at it for a second, then folded it neatly and put it into his own jacket pocket.

I hoped he'd be able to use it.

I hoped it a hell of a lot.

Chapter 24

I WALKED INTO THE Schenectady Diner across from City Hall, and Cardon was sitting in his usual spot. Again.

Except when he saw me. Then he looked at me, disgusted, and started ramming his things in his case. Again.

"Cardon, fancy meeting you here."

"Look, Devin, I just want to get some work done. You've already cost me some time."

I liked the sound of that. "What do you mean? Did you check the file?"

"Yeah," he said, still shoving things, "I managed to squeeze it in — while I was supposed to be doing other work."

"What did you find?"

Cardon stopped, and didn't look too pleased. Only this time it wasn't at me. "There wasn't a lot there."

About what I had found in Streck's file.

"They didn't check a lot else once they had White."

"That's what I was telling you."

Cardon sighed. "What do you want me to do about it, Devin? There's nothing I really can. It's a closed case."

"One that needs to be opened again."

"I have nothing; I can't reopen the case. And you're not giving me anything else here."

"I have Louis Gold. You know who that is?"

Cardon looked at me with a slight cock to his head. "Of course I do. What does he have to do with it?"

Well, at least I had him interested. "As soon as I visited Dee and Dumb… sorry — Price and Black — I had a visitor from Golden Pictures. Their PR man. Offering me work if I would drop the case."

Cardon stood there looking at me, and he wasn't headed for the door. I took that as a good sign. "Then I was called into Golden Pictures by Louis himself. He as much as offered me a bank if I would stop investigating, and at the end of it, he seemed to be making a threat if I didn't."

"Devin, I can't do anything with that and you know it. It's… all in your mind."

"Well, I'm going to prove it."

"If you do, then we can talk."

"That's all I ask, Cardon. Well, there's one other thing…"

Cardon frowned and headed for the door.

I caught up with him and escorted him out. "Once I have the evidence, I'll need you to call Judge James. You know him? He says he knows you. Says you're a good man, apparently."

Cardon stopped, the sharp, setting LA sun casting a golden light on him. "I know the judge. What do you want?"

"Just be open tomorrow." I took out a business card that I had taken from Gramp's desk when I left. It had the judge's number on it. I slipped it into Cardon's front jacket pocket. "I'll call you as soon as I have anything. Then you'll just need to call the judge."

"Just like that?"

"Well, I've never done this before. I had hoped you had an idea of how this was supposed to go." I smiled, but I think it fell on deaf ears.

"You know you've got a real *set*, Devin."

"I know. And if it takes me a bit longer than I thought, the judge will be at Toots' in the evening. You can call him there."

Cardon shook his head, grunted out something that sounded like half a laugh, and headed for the door.

I called out after him. "I'll call you. Tomorrow."

He waved his hand above his head. "I'm looking forward to it." And his back was the last thing I saw as he headed out the door.

And I actually, for the very first time that day, was a slightly happy man.

Chapter 25

I HAD SPENT THE early evening at the office, trying to go over whatever was in Streck's file to see if there was anything actually in there that I could use.

There wasn't. Or maybe there was and I was just too tired to recognize it. So I decided to do the only other thing I could think to do at this point.

I was pretty delirious, and I hated that word, as I drove along Hollywood Boulevard. It was a beautiful state where I didn't really know where I was, but knew where I was. Complete lack of sleep.

It was like the car was floating on air, and I think my brain was, too.

Back in France I'd gone for long days without sleeping, but I think my body now was finally rejecting it all.

Back then it was easy. The enemy was in front of you and you shot him.

Around here, though, it wasn't.

You never were really sure who was the enemy and who wasn't. The only thing you had was what you believed, and you pretty well better hang onto that for all you were worth.

I believed Miles was innocent, and everything I'd heard about Gold, and heard him say out of his own mouth, led me to believe he was the one who did it. Or at least ordered it. Or maybe did it.

And what I learned in the war was, ultimately, you could only really trust yourself. So I was going with it.

And tired or not, delirious or not, I was heading to see if I could push a little harder at Gold and see what shook loose.

It was another thing I learned in the war. An old technique. You lobbed some shells into a trench to see what would come out. If it was guys, the Germans, you shot 'em dead and called it a day. And if it was only rats, sometimes you shot them, too. Because in the end you had to shoot something. You had to make something pay for why you were there.

It's what it got down to in the end.

So I suppose there was a third thing I learned over there: never give up.

The road was blocked ahead and I knew why, so I cut up La Brea to Franklin and then back down Orange to get as close to Hollywood Boulevard as I could. And it was close.

It was a small residential area with neat-kept houses, most of them the white stucco variety, with short green bushes and rose hedges separating the yards. A little farther back up Orange and across Franklin were the hills, where some of the stars lived. A sleepy little area, Hollywood, a small subset of Los Angeles that was made up of homes, a few businesses along Hollywood Boulevard, and of course studios sprinkled around. A quiet place except when they wanted to celebrate themselves. And that's what they were doing right now, and where I was headed.

To a celebration.

Of sorts.

I walked down quiet Orange and could already hear the commotion ahead. A real hubbub.

I got to Hollywood Boulevard and the twelve story Garfield Hotel across the way, but my target was to the left. On my side of the street.

123

Hollywood Boulevard was empty, at least of cars, but people were stacked up five deep on either side of the street, and all of them talking. And all of them looking down toward the lights — the ones stabbing straight up into the sky. The dark, dark sky above us all.

A movie premier.

They'd stopped traffic on Hollywood Boulevard down the way to let all the studio hotshots in. And the stars. Although I knew at least one of them wasn't going to be making it tonight. Because she was dead.

It was Liliana McGann's last movie.

And even by Hollywood's standards, this was a regular zoo.

I pushed my way up the sidewalk, heading to the lights ahead.

There were men and women, all in hats, crowded together, all in coats against the cool night air. At least with my six feet of height I could see over them to the scene ahead.

It was the Moroccan Theater, the queen of Hollywood movie palaces, and cars were bunched right at the great arched entrance to the place.

The Moroccan Theater on the west end of Hollywood was the more rich cousin to Liliana's restaurant on the other side of town. There had been a small dustup when Liliana and her partners had opened their restaurant and seemed to copy the look of the Moroccan here. The Moroccan's owner, Sal Prentiss, made a big stink at the time. I guess he wanted to keep the whole Moroccan theme to himself, but he didn't need to worry about anything. Anyone coming to Hollywood knew the Moroccan was the be-all and end-all of all of Hollywood.

Like a scene from Arabian Nights, the Moroccan rose up off Hollywood Boulevard a full sixty feet at its center. Set back from the boulevard itself, it was completely open in front, except for a giant arched and open gateway standing next to the road. Sal knew that to wall off this place would be to shut out the crowds. So he set the theater itself off the street, with a great courtyard out front, complete with two lit fountains to either side, and the courtyard itself made up of large pieces of poured concrete that he had invited all the biggest and best stars to lay out their footprints, hand prints, and in the case of one starlet with a rather famous appetite for gin, the print of a backside she left after she fell in.

The main building itself rose up peaked and minareted, in perfect Arabian splendor, its false windows and giant doorways trimmed at the edges with masonry lace that would have made a sultan weep.

The great open gateway out front, right at the edge of the sidewalk, rose up to announce the place with sand colored minarets on either side of it, and a large walkway running between them, thirty feet in the air. Usually empty, the walkway tonight was arrayed with a dozen of the Moroccan's trademark gold-turbaned "guards" standing watch over everything, their giant gold-tipped axes resting on white-robed shoulders.

All in all, it was a little much for me; but it really played for the tourists.

And I guess, with a Depression going on, it gave people something to look at besides the day's headlines. Or their empty cupboards.

Anything for the masses.

I wasn't here to see the picture, although it would be interesting to see how they worked around Liliana. Seemed to me if someone was dead you should just let them lie, but that didn't seem to stop Gold.

But I guess, with me, I was doing the same thing. Because with Miles about to die for something I was pretty sure he didn't do, I wasn't going to let it lie either.

So in the great tradition of rattling cages, I decided it was some kind of good idea to come to the premiere tonight. And lob some shells.

After all, Max had invited me, right?

An empty black Duesenberg Phaeton drove past on the Boulevard to my right, its driver in full livery. I think it was a law in Hollywood that, whenever they blocked off a street for premieres, only the best cars were allowed on. I laughed. I would like to see my gunmetal blue Ford Model A roll down the road right next to the Duesenbergs, Lincolns, and Cadillacs.

It wouldn't stand a chance.

Ahead, the crowd that was already thick got even thicker.

There was an opening in the crowd right in front of the Moroccan, a kind of Moses-parting-the-Red-Sea area where the cops had roped off the hoi polloi to let all the Hollywood swells out of their cars. My guess was the only thing red there was the carpet under their feet. And I'll bet it was thick, too.

At the edge of the sidewalk, another large car coughed out its occupants, all of them tumbling out in mink stoles, black tuxedos, and cigars. A couple of cheers went up as the crowd recognized somebody; all of them, on both sides of the police rope, happy and glad, waving, with smiles all around. Someone escorted the latest batch of swells from the edge of the sidewalk down toward a nest of microphones, where they all stopped dutifully to talk to a rather energetic young man dressed in his own little penguin suit.

I recognized him as Walter Hoagland. The king of gossip in a land that ran on it. Not my kind of guy.

As I finally got to the edge of the police rope, I saw Max, in a tuxedo, on the other side of the sidewalk. He was handling logistics like he was handling a war. I knew he'd served and you could see it by the way he carried himself. Nothing stopped him and he took everything as it came. Although with the smile that he always seemed to carry, I didn't know that I could picture him shooting anybody. But I'm sure he did. Everyone did over there.

Max finished with one set of swells at the microphone and sent them on toward the great red wooden doors of the theater itself and headed himself toward a large Cadillac just pulling up at the street. I tried to catch him before he left. "Max!"

Max looked up and saw me across the line. He looked back at the Cadillac, then came for me instead. Maybe he was a good judge of character. "I didn't think you'd come."

"I didn't think I would either, but somehow the car just got me here." Which was the truth.

"You look like hell."

Which was the truth, too. "Maybe you should be a detective, Max. You're good at it."

Max laughed, then nodded for me to come in under the rope. I ducked under, to the catcalls of a few of the people I left behind, who wanted to come along themselves for the party.

The carpet really was thick. And red. And clean.

Like nobody had ever used it.

Only the best for our little Liliana.

Or was it for all the swells themselves? More like that, I decided. They couldn't care less who they were coming to see. They just wanted to walk on that carpet and remind themselves how important they were.

Or maybe that was just me being a cynic.

At least I could breathe on the carpet, the air open and swirling just a bit with the breeze. The breeze hadn't even registered with me before. Nothing much registered lately. I was too tired.

Max pointed to a deep blue Rolls-Royce with a black top pulling up to the curb. "I've got to get this."

"I'm not going anywhere."

He ran off while I stood in the middle of the red carpet, the only one in a brown suit on this side of the police rope.

It was strange for me, being on the inside. A lot of people on the other side of the rope looked at me like they were trying to figure out who I was. Thinking I was somebody. I wanted to tell them I was nobody, but I didn't even have the energy to do that.

A couple of the photographers racing up and down the carpet flicked their eyes at me as they ran past, wondering if I was anybody. But looking at my ten-dollar suit was enough for them. And they didn't give me another look after that.

Max walked back to me after doing his duties opening the car door. The guy he helped out of the car wore a monocle on his left eye, and a penguin suit below that was trying hard to push in his big belly. He also wore white spats down below that looked like something out of the last century. I smiled as Max came up and motioned with my chin to the guy. "Who's the muckety-muck?"

Max didn't even look back. "Gold's business partner."

"I didn't know he had a partner."

"It's not common knowledge. The studios are owned mostly out of New York."

I looked at Max like the sleep-deprived idiot that I was. "I never heard of that."

"Nobody does. And everybody wants it that way."

"So why'd you tell me?"

Max smiled. "I don't know. Maybe I like honesty."

I laughed. "Then why the hell are you doing PR?"

Max thought for a bit and instead of his usual smile, something settled in him deep down. "Honestly, I had to get some kind of job."

"And this is what you settled for?"

His eyebrows arched up and his mouth cocked to the side. "Beggars can't be choosers. Not in this day and time anyway. Besides," Max smiled then, "I get to work on the lot and be surrounded by a lot of pretty women."

"There is that."

And there was. I couldn't help but notice all of them traipsing in on the arms of the men in the tuxedos, and few of the younger men traipsing in on the arms of the women. All of them were beautiful. If you liked beautiful.

Max seemed like an okay sort. Not the kind to beat around the bush, even if he did walk around with a smile on his face and a job that required him to spout bull. After all, he said he liked honesty. So I thought I'd test him. "Would Gold have wanted Liliana dead?"

There it was, out. Out there like a guy in a brown suit in the middle of a red carpet.

The smile dropped off Max's mug and he stared at me like I had just called into question his mother's integrity. "I don't even know how to answer that."

"You might try honestly." Not trying to throw his own words back at him. But I was. And I was a PI. We threw a lot of things around.

I think he was a little thrown off by the question, but he jumped in admirably. "Why do you even ask that?"

"Why? Because I think he did it. Or had it done. But like I said, do you think he did it?"

Max shook his head to get the cobwebs out, or whatever was blocking whatever was in there. I wasn't sure if he was trying to come up with an answer, an excuse, or… "No. And that's a ridiculous question."

"What's a ridiculous question?"

The voice was unmistakable. I turned to face Gold himself, Stan standing two steps behind. Gold looked good in his tuxedo, like he belonged in it. Stan, on the other hand, looked… even harder in it. Like the black of it was a knife that could cut through any kind of color that dared stand around him.

I smiled at the both of them. A cheap brown suit in the middle of all that royalty. "I was just asking Max here if he thought Miles killed Liliana."

A small shade of a look passed over Gold's sharp eyes, like everything inside of him had gone blank. Like a cold piece of steel. Then, just as quickly, the regular hardness snapped back into his eyes, and the man in charge was there. With the smallest of smirks planted on the corner of his mouth. "And what did he say?"

Gold didn't even look at Max. He just looked at me and I could feel the energy radiating off him like a car engine redlining, but everything was quiet. Everything was still. Everything was peaceful. I shrugged my shoulders. "Nothing. He said nothing." Then I smiled. "Because you came up."

Gold then looked over at Max and Max took the stare he was given. Gold lowered his voice to a whisper. A whisper as ragged and hard as a piece of broken glass. "Well?"

Max simply stood there, the three of us forming a triangle on the red carpet with Stan immediately behind Gold. But Max most decidedly between Gold and me.

Max smiled coolly. "If the police arrested him, Devin — that seems to be good enough for me."

Max hadn't moved and hadn't even so much as breathed. He wasn't scared of Gold, that was for sure, but maybe he needed to be. In France, the battlefields were littered with shells that had been tossed but had never gone off. They were always the worst. You could never quite predict when, or if, any of them would go off. So in addition to the Germans, we shot them, too.

They made big explosions. They were fun to watch.

As long as you weren't anywhere near them.

Gold turned to face me, his big body solidly placed between Max and me. "I like you, Devin. I don't know why, but I do." He waved at a lesser starlet walking past, holding her black-gloved hand on the arm of yet another swell in a tuxedo. Then Gold turned back to face me. "I think there's something hard inside of you that likes to get things done."

"I do."

"Good. Then work for me. You'll be glad you did."

I had my doubts about that. "I'll let you know what I'm thinking."

Without a word, Gold turned and Stan followed him toward the great red wooden doors held open to the theater beyond.

As they walked I saw Stan nod. Once. I heard nothing, and Gold's head never once bent down to say anything into Stan's ear, but I guess that's the way it was with the king. He spoke, and people listened.

Too bad I made it a habit to go against what everyone told me. My old man always said it was a stubborn streak. Usually before he beat me.

But me? I always liked to think of it as a healthy sense of stick you.

It hadn't gotten me killed yet.

But it had gotten me in more than a few interesting situations.

"I could have answered for myself."

I turned to Max and he didn't seem mad, just… solid. "I know you could have." Then I nodded to him. "I have to get going. Even though you believe Miles did it, I tend to think otherwise."

"I didn't say I thought that, you did."

I smiled. "And I said it just to hear how crazy it sounded. Have a great time tonight." I looked up at a great poster plastered to the courtyard wall with Liliana, bigger than life, looking down on us. She wore a frilly blue dress and smiled, and she had a screwy look on her face like everything was going to be all right. I looked back at Max. "I hope she was worth it."

Then I walked back to the police rope, ducked under, and joined my own kind on the other side of it.

I had work to do.

Chapter 26

I WALKED DOWN THE hall to my office and could smell it. Coffee.

Bella.

I opened the door and, sure enough, the smell of it hit me square in the face. She'd made coffee and left it on the hot plate for me. I walked over and picked up the pot. Full.

No matter what I thought of Bella, no matter how many times I wanted to kill her, and I'm sure she wanted to kill me too, she was okay.

I walked into my office and grabbed a mug out of my lower drawer and, while I was there, I saw my bottle of whiskey. I pulled that out too and set it on the desk. Just in case.

I went out to the hotplate and the bucket of joe sitting on top of it, and poured myself a mug. Leaving a little room for something fun.

It had been a long day and it was going to be a long night. After stopping by the premier, my anger was up so I didn't feel too tired anymore. Maybe it was because the adrenaline was going. Or maybe it was because I was too stupid to think of anything else.

But I felt wide awake.

I set the mug of coffee down on my desk, down on the blotter, right next to my drool mark from this morning. They looked good sitting next to each other. The mug of joe and the drool.

But what looked even better was the bottle sitting next to both of them.

I poured a little of the whiskey into the coffee, then picked up a loose pencil lying on the desk and stirred it all up. Then I licked the pencil. It was good. No use letting anything go to waste.

I pulled out a big pad of paper and sat down. I always thought better when I wrote things out.

So I wrote four names along the top of the pad: Daisy, James, Dante, and Gold. I underlined each one a couple of times just to give them some weight. I was awake all right, but I wanted to make sure I wasn't missing anything.

I started by adding things under each name at random. That let my mind wander, which it liked to do, but the columns kept what I wrote all neat and tidy.

As I looked at the four names, I knew it had to be one of them. Because if it wasn't, I did not have the time to find another needle in this very messy haystack.

I looked at my strap watch and it was eleven thirty… in twenty-four hours they would be prepping Miles. Maybe he'd have his last meal. Maybe he wouldn't. I can't imagine I'd be able to hold anything down when I knew they were coming for me.

So I got to work.

Gold was high on my list and, to be honest, I figured it was him did it. Or caused it to be done. Stan looked the type. To do what he was told. And enjoy it.

So Daisy and James…

James just plain didn't have it in him, I thought. He was too browbeat by Daisy and, probably, the same happened from Liliana.

Now Daisy, she had the anger — in spades — but…

I made a note to the right of the calendar in our little shorthand, for Bella to check Daisy and James, and see if they had any police records. The side of the calendar was full of the little notes, most of them crossed off, this one fresh and new.

I had half an idea that Daisy would have a record, just because of her former employment — you don't operate as a prostitute in this town without getting arrested at least a few times — but if there was anything more violent than picking up johns, I'd be surprised.

I hadn't listed Liliana on the pad but probably should have. I'm sure she gave enough other people a lot of excuses to want to kill her, at least based on what I'd heard just from these four. But from what was said, Liliana had pretty much gone off on all of them — including Miles — that night, and the one thing murder is usually about — is passion. And not the romantic kind. The kind where people get so enraged they do something about it. And Liliana had pretty much done that to all of them. Enraged them. Well, I couldn't speak for all of them, but she'd given enough people an excuse to come after her.

Unless I was wrong about Daisy and James, that left me with Dante and Gold. And I already had my feelings about Gold.

I looked at Dante's name and wrote under it "kicked out the gambling" and… nothing else. But that one thing alone would have been enough to get anyone killed. Just on principle. But the lighter that was found in the restaurant was such an obvious plant that it was almost comical. And the only reason Dee and Dumb didn't go after Dante was because the "M" matched Miles. Of all the things. Dumb luck. At least as far as I could see it. Dee and Dumb luck.

Under Gold's name I wrote "contract," and then "Max."

Max seemed like an okay enough guy but you can never be sure. Stan seemed like more the one who would have done it, killed Liliana, but I'd seen a lot of guys do a lot of things for a paycheck. But the problem was more that he had just shown up out of the blue earlier, right after I had gone to see Dee and Dumb.

Now maybe I should have added their names to the pad, too. They were obviously in on it, but my guess was only to swing the charges away from somebody. And onto Miles as it turned out.

Or the charges could have just as easily been on Dante.

And if Dante wanted anything done about Liliana, he would have done it himself and dared the cops to come after him. Dante was nothing if not un-subtle.

Then I added "contract" under Dante's column, because he was helping Liliana with it. And that, in anybody's book, would have been a great reason for Gold to drop a lighter with an *M* on it at the murder scene. Which meant it was premeditated.

Hmm… maybe not as much passion as I thought, which meant that Gold had—

The outside door to the office opened, and I quick reached for one of my guns.

I held it in front of me, below my desk.

I looked through my open office door to the opening outer door, and in walked Tweedle-Dee and Tweedle-Dumb.

Dee was in the lead and he smiled at me as he came toward my office door, followed by Dumb. "Working late?"

His smile looked like upturned lips on a snake.

I still kept the gun below. I didn't trust these two any further than I could shoot them. "So I guess we have a lot in common. You two and me. Working late. Unless this is a social visit. In which case I'm sorry, but I never got around to baking you a cake."

Dumb laughed. Then Dee swung his face around and sneered at him.

Dumb got quiet fast.

It was the little ones you always had to worry about.

I looked at the both of them, standing in the doorway to my office. "Is there anything I can help you gentlemen with?"

Dee looked at Dumb. "You hear that, he called us gentlemen."

Dumb looked… just dumb. "I did for a fact."

He must have heard that somewhere and copied it, because using "fact" in a sentence sure didn't seem like something Dumb would even attempt on his own.

Dee swung his dark eyes back to me. "What are you doin'?"

"Trying to save a life. You should try it sometime."

They both sauntered in and Dee sat in one of the chairs in front of my desk, while Dumb kept himself standing, right behind the other one. As they settled they both looked around the office, specifically at all the safes. They thankfully didn't say anything. I was tired of explaining the safes to everyone who asked.

I still had the gun below the desk, but this wasn't the time I wanted to use it. It would probably end up in me dying. Either one of them would nail me, or I'd be in the same place as Miles, but I'd get there a lot quicker, killing a couple of cops. "Just to let you know I have a gun under here and I'm going to pull it out."

Dumb pulled his gun from his jacket pocket, fumbled it out more like, but Dee sat there coolly. Apparently I didn't scare him.

"I'm only telling you because I want to put it away. Because I like you guys."

Dumb kept his gun on me while I grabbed my gun by the front end, well away from the trigger, and dropped it into the lower desk drawer and shut it — the gun safely where it belonged. At least when you had two less than honest cops in front of you. My guess was they were looking for any reason to lock me up. Or worse.

Or worse... Okay, I was way too tired. That should have popped into my head a lot faster than it just had.

Now I wondered if they were here for more than talking, and more like killing.

I started having second thoughts about dropping that gun.

Dumb still had his gun pointed right at my eyes, and there'd be no way I could get to mine fast enough. I put both of my hands up onto my desk in plain sight, and grabbed the pencil sitting there. I fiddled with the pencil just to occupy myself, and also let them know that I wasn't going for the gun. At least for now. "Just to let you know I was trying to be honest with you boys. See, that's where you tell the truth about something. It actually feels good when you do it. Because you don't have to remember things up inside your head, like the lies you told people."

Dee looked at me with that same hardness in his eyes and I

recognized it. It came from carrying a badge for a long time. "Think you're smart? Now let me ask something here." Dee looked over at Dumb, "Didn't we tell him not to look into this?"

Dumb smiled a nice satisfied smile. Like he was a kid eating ice cream. "Yup."

"See, that's what I thought." Then Dee looked back over at me. "So what are we supposed to do if you don't do what we tell you to?"

"Well, I suppose you could shoot me if you want."

Dee laughed, and he was actually happy. "Don't tempt me, Devin. It's a thought a lot of us have had."

"That include Cardon?"

Dee's face went blank. "I don't care what that guy thinks or wants." Then he reached behind his back and came around the side of the desk.

"What are you guys doing?!" I don't normally shout, but I did to get their attention.

"Shut up!" Dumb pushed his gun a couple of inches closer to me.

Dee looked at him. "If you need to shoot him, just don't hit me."

Dumb smiled, as the pencil in my hand scratched out a couple of cryptic lines and squiggles at the edge of my calendar.

My brain was full of cotton and I didn't look down at my pencil, so I only hoped what I wrote, Bella could figure out. Then I casually laid the pencil down.

Unfortunately, it caught Dee's attention. "What's that?"

I looked up at him next to me. "What's what?"

"That there." He pointed to my scratches.

I looked down at them. And they were barely legible. Even to me. My heart sank. "Those there?"

Dee looked from the marks back to me. He now had his own gun out with the cuffs still in his other hand. I hoped I got the cuffs. Dee nodded, his eyes now hooded. "Yeah."

I smiled. I hoped it didn't look as strained as it was. "I doodle when I get nervous."

"Doodle?"

Dumb snickered. "'Did he say he doodled?" Then he looked at me. "You should have gone to the bathroom instead of doing it in your chair."

Dee's face read exactly what he was thinking of Dumb — seven-eighths short of a load. Then Dee's eyes traveled from my doodles, over to the pad of paper sitting on top of the desk calendar. He read the names there, and didn't actually move his mouth when he did.

Confirmed. He definitely was the smarter of the two.

Dee ripped off the sheet with Daisy, James, Dante, and Gold's names on it, crumbled it up, and stuffed it in his jacket pocket. "You won't be needing that."

I looked him in the eye so I could see. "Which one of them is paying you? Gold?"

Dee gave me a swift backhand with the butt of his gun to the side of my head.

I almost went down but stayed up to spite him.

He put his gun away, then pulled one of my arms up and shot the handcuffs around that wrist, then leaned down and did the same to the other. The click of metal was satisfying. To at least two of the people in the room. Not to me.

"There," Dee smiled at me, "that wasn't so bad, was it?"

"So where are you taking me?"

"Why? You worried?" Dee's laugh didn't make me feel too good.

"No, I just want to know if I should change into something a little nicer."

"Relax. For some reason someone finds you interesting. So you're just going to sit on ice for a while."

"Let me guess, until after midnight tomorrow?"

The smile dropped off Dee's face, and he just picked me up by the cuffs and led me out of my own office.

Of course it will be until after tomorrow. After that, no one would care. Miles would already be dead and if I did raise a stink that there had been some kind of mistake? Well, it was in everyone's best interest to keep it quiet. Everyone's at that point.

Except, of course, Miles'.

I couldn't believe how badly I'd blown it, and in my exhausted mind, somehow wished I would have really opened up on them with my gun.

Then maybe I would have had a chance at saving Miles. But like I said, then it would be me going for the noose.

Either way I was headed for sleep, which on the one hand felt good. But on the other, maybe it was the kind of sleep you didn't wake up from.

Ever.

And that I definitely did not like.

Chapter 27

BELLA WALKED INTO THE office to the smell of very burned coffee.

She dropped her purse on her desk and walked over to the hot plate that was still — hot.

She checked the pot and the level was down a bit, so Devin had been here, but it wasn't like him to not turn off the hotplate when he left. Unless...

Bella smiled, and walked toward the open door to his office. "All right Sleeping Beauty, it's time—"

But there was nobody in his office. And the desk lamp was still lit.

An empty pad of paper lay in the middle of his desk calendar and a coffee cup, mostly full. She sniffed at the cup and could smell the whiskey. He was definitely there last night. At least he hadn't started drinking in the morning and... Bella sighed. She wasn't his mother.

He must have left fast enough, that he forgot to turn off the hotplate — and finish his Irish coffee.

Then Bella looked down at the lower right corner of the

calendar and the series of symbols there. Their shorthand.

Their code.

Whenever he needed something and he didn't want anyone else to know what it was about.

A pretty handy thing when you had a detective agency.

The marks were there as clear as a bell, and they hadn't been there when she left last night.

Five marks in total — a dot, then a vertical line, then a small circle with a line through it and next to that, two squiggly lines.

The dot meant that it was related to a current case. The vertical line meant trouble. The circle with the line meant the cops. And the two squiggly lines — meant coffee. Which made absolutely no sense at all.

But then she looked closer. They were *D*s. Two *D*s.

There was only one set of *D*s she knew that were cops, if it was what Devin was trying to tell her: Tweedle-Dee and Tweedle-Dumb.

Bella picked up the phone and dialed.

The cavalry.

And prayed that he would come.

Chapter 28

IT WAS TWELVE IN the afternoon by the time Cardon got fed up. He'd searched every precinct, every place he could think of. And had come up with nothing.

It was an old cop trick if you wanted to get rid of someone. You locked them up and threw away the proverbial key. At least for a little while until you were ready to let them go. And Cardon figured that would be after midnight tonight.

If they were in on the McGann/White case, and judging by the case file he had looked at he had a pretty good idea they were, he didn't want to tip his hat that he was looking for Devin. That would only get him moved, or worse.

But Cardon had spent the entire morning looking at all the usual locations, and there was nothing. No Devin. And the White kid had less than twelve hours to live, so Cardon was fed up. Very fed up, as a matter of fact, as he walked into the detective room, ready to break a couple of heads.

Price and Black stood in the back, laughing at some joke one of them had told.

Cardon walked down the aisle past all the other detectives,

who did a great job of ignoring him. Fine.

Cardon kept the rage he felt in check, at least for the moment. As he got to Price and Black, the smiles on their faces dropped as soon as he walked up. "Have a question for you boys. It's on a case. You have a second?" Then he turned away from them and headed back up the aisle. He was afraid if he waited he'd have already pulled his gun.

That would wait.

Price and Black looked at each other, then followed Cardon.

Out in the hall, Cardon opened the door to another office. This one was small, and had no windows. Nothing to distract, and nobody to see. They used it for interrogations.

Cardon held the door open as Price and Black walked inside, then Cardon followed them in.

"What's this about?" Price asked, his beady black eyes not sure what was up, and not entirely trusting Cardon.

Nobody liked Cardon, none of the detectives.

The feeling was mutual.

Black stood near the corner. Cardon thought he looked like a big kid there, afraid maybe he was caught at something. Price? Nothing but coldness.

Cardon smiled, stepped in toward Price, then pulled his gun and shoved the barrel into Price's mouth.

Price's small eyes went big as Black stumbled back all the way into the corner, trying to pull something out of his jacket pocket.

"Don't, Black." Cardon looked at him long enough to stop Black dead in his tracks, his hand still in his jacket pocket. "Pull your hand out, empty." Cardon looked back into Price's eyes. "And you, don't move a muscle or I will pull the trigger. And the warning is more than what you deserve."

Black didn't listen and leveled his gun at Cardon, his arm shaking.

"Black," Cardon kept his voice calm. "I told you to pull it out empty. Now why did you go and do that?" Cardon hoped Black wasn't stupid enough to actually pull the trigger.

Cardon looked back into the small black eyes of Price, and could see he was just as scared as Black. That was good. "Devin. Where did you put him? And you'd better not say he's gone."

"What in the hell, Cardon?" Black's voice shook just like his hands did, the barrel of his gun dancing two inches in every direction. He tried to laugh, but it came out as a choking sound. "What do you mean about Devin?" Black tried to throw in a smile, too.

It didn't work. Cardon didn't even acknowledge Black. The guy was too stupid to do anything. "Black… if you don't put that gun away, I'm gonna blow Price's head off right here. And I am not lying."

Black looked back and forth between Cardon and Price. Then lowered his weapon.

Cardon felt a little bit of sweat form at the back of his neck. "Good job, Black. This is only going to take a second, because Price's going to tell me exactly what I want to know." Cardon looked back at Price, directly into his eyes. "Now I'm going to pull this gun out of your mouth, and I'm gonna put it right up to your forehead. That way, with an open mouth, you can tell me what I want to hear. Do you understand?"

Cardon watched as the fear in Price's eyes turned to anger. It didn't bother Cardon one bit. He kept thinking back to all the cases he should be working on right now. "I'm telling you, Price, don't even think of trying anything; you took him and I know it. I don't care who's paying you what, I don't care who's got what on you, I just want to know where Devin is. Easy, right? Then I'm going to go get him, and I'm going to talk him out of trying to kill you both. Because he will do it."

Even though Price had a badge and used it, Cardon could see that it was sinking in that yes, Devin was probably good for it.

Price swallowed hard, and nodded.

Cardon nodded back. "Good job."

Cardon pulled the gun out of Price's mouth and, just as he said, slid the short barrel straight into the center of Price's forehead.

"Now talk."

Price took a couple of breaths to calm himself down, then on his last exhale he gave it up, "Pasadena."

No wonder Cardon hadn't found Devin. Pasadena was outside LAPD jurisdiction. Maybe Price and Black were smarter than he thought. Or at least Price was. "Good. Now I'm going to go get him, and we're going to forget that I had this little conversation with you both. But if you ever come back at me for this, I will kill you," Cardon looked over at Black, "…both."

With that, Cardon pulled the gun away from Price's forehead, put it back in his belt holster, and left.

Out in the marbled hallway, Cardon looked down at his watch. It was twelve thirty in the afternoon. Less than twelve hours until the kid would be hanged.

He got to his car and drove.

Chapter 29

THE DRIVE UP TO Pasadena took half an hour.

Cardon knew his little meeting with Black and Price would cost him. Like it had cost him every other time before. Any other time he stood up and tried to do what was right.

They all hated him. He didn't have a partner, and he probably never would. He tried to keep his head down as much as he could, but sometimes he just couldn't keep out of it. When he saw something that wasn't right, he tended to do something about it. And then paid for it.

It was like that in the war, too. You told people something they didn't want to hear, and they tended to not listen to you again. Or worse. Like shuffle you off to a trench somewhere to lead charges. Where you wouldn't come back from.

But Cardon did come back, and sometimes he wondered if it was all even worth it.

The Pasadena city jail was a small place, but the cells were strong enough. The cop out front was reluctant, but Cardon kept walking past him into the back of the jail where he found Devin in the third cell on the left. Laid out like he was dead.

But Cardon saw his chest rising and falling, so he at least knew he wasn't dead. Bella'd be happy about that. "You have a nice beauty rest?"

Devin's head jerked, then dropped back down to the cot. Then it slowly lifted and turned to look at Cardon. It was like his eyes couldn't focus.

"You look like hell." And he did, Cardon thought, like they had beat him or something. Not because of any bruises, but because of the way he looked at Cardon. Like his brain hadn't engaged yet. And maybe never would.

"Come on out…" The cop from out front yelled, resigned to having to actually do this. He shoved the key into the cell lock, threw it, and opened up the door with a loud screech. "Come on, get outta there! Apparently you got big-time friends."

The cop walked into the cell with Devin, then kicked at the edge of the cot next to Devin's face. "Up and at 'em, sunshine!"

Cardon watched as Devin's eyes slowly began to register… something. He did look like hell.

Devin managed to get up slow, and finally upright, his hands gripped onto the edge of the cot to help him get oriented. Then he got up slow, as if finally remembering what his legs were for. Devin's eyes swiveled up to Cardon and they finally hit something. Recognition. "Fancy meeting you here."

"Come on…" The cop was impatient and hooked an arm under Devin's, then lifted him to his feet.

Devin's legs finally caught and he tentatively headed for the cell door and through it.

Cardon reached out for Devin's arm and took it, trying to help him.

Devin looked down at it. "We going to dance?"

Cardon didn't need this. He didn't need any of it. "No. And shut up."

They made it out to the sidewalk outside the jail. It was hot out there. It always was in Pasadena.

A few cops walked past heading left and right, but nobody

paid them much attention. Except a couple that eyed Cardon like he didn't belong there. Well, he didn't.

Devin looked at Cardon. "Thanks for getting me out."

"Did they hit you?"

Devin looked at Cardon like he still didn't understand what was going on.

"Do you even understand me?"

Devin started to finally track. He shook his head. "No. Nothing. As soon as they got me here, I was out. I haven't slept in a few days."

"How many?"

Devin looked up at the sky. He was fascinated by it. "What day is it?"

"Thursday."

"Then that would make it three."

Cardon whistled. "You get any in there?"

Devin looked back at Cardon. "I tried yelling for a while, but when that didn't work, and I never expected it to, I laid down. Then I heard your sweet voice."

Cardon grunted. "I'll take you back to your office. Bella's been worried."

Devin sighed. "What time is it?"

"About one. A little after."

"Thursday, and it's one. So Miles is still alive?"

"For eleven more hours."

Devin considered that. "I'm even more sure it was Gold."

"You got anything on him yet?"

"No. But give me a little time." Devin stopped for a bit, looking down at the sidewalk. Then he looked back up at Cardon. "You were in the war, right, Cardon?"

Cardon wasn't sure where the question came from. And wasn't exactly sure he wanted to follow it down. A lot of water under that bridge. He nodded to Devin.

Devin nodded back. "I guess I've been out of the Marines for so long, I forgot what it was like to have someone next to you."

Cardon looked at Devin, rumpled and, from what it looked like, barely alive. And Cardon understood.

"Thanks for coming for me."

Cardon wasn't sure that he could smile, but he did the next best thing. He nodded. Short, and to the point.

Devin nodded back at him. "You up for helping a little more on this?"

Cardon couldn't believe it. He'd just spent the whole morning looking for Devin, and now he was supposed to keep on going? Like he didn't have anything else to do? "You mean more than I have already?"

Devin smiled. "That's what I thought. Thanks."

"I didn't agree to anything."

"You didn't have to." Devin started walking up the sidewalk. "Now where's your car? I think I could use a ride back to my office."

Cardon scratched the side of his face, then slipped his hand over his jaw, working it back and forth. It was an old response, part frustration and part nervousness. He always got that way when he didn't know what was coming.

And with this whole situation, Cardon didn't know what was coming at all.

Chapter 30

I WALKED INTO THE office and immediately Charlie jumped up from his Coca-Cola card table in the corner. Bella just sat at her desk, her eyes focused on me, and I saw a large breath escape her. She looked like hell.

"You look like hell." She said it to me. And I felt it.

Then from the corner of my eye, I noticed… "Mrs. White."

Miles' mother rose slowly, with great effort, from the chair she had been waiting in. It looked like it took everything she had just to get out of that chair.

Her son was due to be hanged in only a few hours.

She looked right at me. "I've been waiting a bit, Mr. Devin. I wanted to say what I had to say once you were here, too."

"She's been waiting for a while." Bella offered.

Then Mrs. White made it a point to look into each of our eyes. "I wanted to come here to wish you all good luck today."

I looked at Bella, and felt like I had been hit in the gut with a hammer.

A tear formed at the corner of Bella's right eye. But it didn't fall.

"Miss Caruso here told me that you've been working all

morning on the case." Mrs. White began.

The hammer took another swing into my middle. I hadn't been working, I had only been sleeping. In a cell.

Mrs. White made it a point to single out Bella and Charlie. "And I know all of you have been working hard for my boy."

Another blow of the hammer. This time to my head. Because I had hardly let them do anything at all.

"I know it has been a lot to ask, me coming like I did yesterday, but I appreciate everything you've done so far. I didn't want to interrupt you, but…" Then she looked right back at me. "I wanted to let you know how much it meant to me. That you're working for my boy."

Bella cleared her throat.

I wanted to clear my whole body.

I felt dirty.

"I'm going back to my hotel room right now, and I would appreciate it very much if you could give me a call if you're able to do anything. And don't you worry how late it is. I will be up."

Mrs. White hadn't stopped talking, not since the moment she opened her mouth. I suppose it was probably to keep me, or any of us, from saying anything back. Anything bad. Or nothing at all.

That was probably worse to her. Nothing at all.

And I had nothing for her.

Mrs. White walked in her short, measured walk to the door and I, like a coward, said nothing.

She reached out a white gloved hand for the door and opened it. "God bless you all."

Then she left.

The door shut with the softest of sounds, and the three of us were left there in the outer office. All of us staring at that door.

I looked up at the clock on the wall and it showed exactly three o'clock. Exactly nine hours until her son would die. Because I couldn't prove that somebody else had done it.

Chapter 31

I STOOD THERE AND couldn't move.

I couldn't think.

And I had no idea what to do.

"We're going to help her, right?"

The voice came from somewhere. Somewhere outside the cotton that seemed to be stuffed inside my own head. I thought I had slept some last night in the cell but I really wasn't sure that I had. And I wasn't sure that it was even enough after being up for two, three, or however many days it was. Honestly, I wasn't even sure if I was conscious anymore.

I looked back around and Bella looked up at me from behind her desk, her brown eyes boring into mine. It was like she was trying to reach in through the haze of my mind.

And slowly I came back out into consciousness.

And found myself standing in the middle of my outer office, with two people staring at me who wanted to know what to do.

I wished I could tell them.

Charlie spoke up again. "We're going to help her, right?"

I looked at him. I loved the kid's innocence. "Sometimes it's not that easy."

"But we can't just quit."

Well, I had never quit before. Ever. And I didn't think I would now. But…

I just couldn't move. I was frozen there.

I had too much to do and there was no time to do it in.

The Hanson case, the Garcia case… and yes, the Miles White case. It was all too much.

I knew I had kept them out of it. Bella and Charlie.

Miles' mother had gotten to me. That sense of loss that I saw in her yesterday when she first came, that she didn't want to admit was about to happen?

I had lost my mother. The only real thing I had. And I never wanted to feel that again.

So I wanted to keep Bella and Charlie safe. Not exposed. Right from the beginning, I guess, and especially now.

I know whoever killed Liliana could come at us — them — but I had probably been afraid of that for a while now. On all of the cases. And that had gotten me here. Backed down finally into a tiny little ball, trying to do it all by myself.

But looking at them standing there, I realized I was like Miles' mother. Only sideways.

She was trying to save Miles, and I was trying to protect them.

And while Bella was definitely not my child and neither was Charlie, they were the closest to family I had right now. Or probably ever would.

And I didn't want them to get hurt.

My lip twitched.

Bella looked at me, and I knew she wanted to do whatever it took. And Charlie, well, he was just plain angry. He had a lot more anger to go through in life before he got to the end of it, but I liked what he wanted to do now. What both of them wanted to do. Which was anything, everything, to save Miles.

Then I remembered back to what I had said to Cardon, what? Maybe an hour ago? About how it felt good to have someone standing next to you.

John Devin Investigations.

I was looking right at it. Them. All of us.

Charlie spoke up, again. "You tell me what I need to do, Mr. Devin. And I'll do it."

Then Bella stood up, still looking at me with those brown eyes of hers. She had been quiet for a long while, and usually, that was the time to watch out. "We still have some time. Not a lot, but we've got it. If you stop being a stubborn, pigheaded, idiot ass and let us help."

Bella looked over at Charlie and he nodded. Then he looked back at me. They both did.

And I nodded. "Okay. Although I don't know what we can do."

"Neither do we," Bella began, "so why don't we go figure it out."

Together. And I liked that.

I liked it a lot.

Chapter 32

I SAT AT MY desk, the calendar in front of me with a cup of coffee on top of it thanks to Bella. Bella and Charlie sat in front of me.

Bella and Charlie both had pads of paper in front of them on my desk, and Bella was interviewing me, like I did to everyone else when I was trying to figure out what was what. "So what have you found out?"

I had to think about it for a little bit. This is all I had been working on for the past day, but it's amazing what a night in jail and three nights of no sleep will do for you. "Okay, I've got Gold, who I think probably did it."

Charlie whistled.

I looked at him. "And nothing leaves this room."

Charlie didn't move, and his eyes didn't leave mine. I think I scared him. Good. He needed to learn to keep his mouth shut.

"I also have her two business partners, Daisy and James." There was something in the back of my head about them and I reached for it. Then I pulled out my little red pad from my jacket and searched, and found it. I looked at Bella, "Check arrest records on

Daisy and James. See if anything comes up violent. I'm guessing not, but see what comes up. If there is, we'll have to decide if I need to get over there and push harder, but my guess is they didn't do anything. Except identify the lighter as Miles'. Which means Gold got to them. If he did it, that is. Because there's also Dante Manzione."

Charlie's eyes snapped to attention. "The real one?"

I looked at him. He really was a kid. But he also had to join the real world. "That's right, the one and only."

Charlie whispered lightly under his breath. It wasn't anything he learned in church. Maybe the real world was going to be a little too much for him. But then he went and surprised me, "Let's get him."

I held in my smile. "Calm down, kid. Dante is not exactly a man you want to go out and *get*."

I felt the weight of my two guns in their shoulder holsters. They felt at least a little reassuring. It's about the only thing that did.

And the two sitting across from me, they felt reassuring, too. Somehow.

"Gold," Bella started. She hadn't stopped writing since I had been talking. I wondered if she had written all the names along the top of her pad like I had. "You think he's the one because of Max stopping by right away?"

She said what I had been thinking.

She had her own cup of coffee in front of her, and I could see the mark of her red lipstick along the top of it. She always wore it. It was like her trademark. Maybe like I wore my guns.

And she was getting her detective's license. I still couldn't believe it.

"John."

I drifted back.

"John…" I made it finally back, and Bella stared at me. "Did you get any sleep last night?"

I thought about it. "Kind of."

She looked up at the wall clock in my office. I was in my office.

"We have less than eleven hours. We have to get this."

"Right. What were you saying?"

"I was asking — do you think Max is in on it?"

I shook my head. Then I shrugged my shoulders. "I don't know. I don't think so, but…"

"Okay, we'll figure it out. So what about Dante?"

I liked how she was asking all around Gold to begin with. Everything else but him. Get rid of the obvious first, then go for the… gold. But I could tell by the way she just said it, she really hoped it wasn't Dante. She understood who he was. She came from the neighborhood.

"He had a gambling operation up in the top of Liliana's restaurant. Liliana's, Daisy's, and James' restaurant. But Liliana had started to make waves about it. And on the night they all had dinner—"

"The night she was killed?"

"Yeah. She told Dante she was gonna kick him out. I think she was cleaning house that night, and that included everyone. Including Miles. I think she was tired of being the gravy train for everyone. Near as I can tell, everyone was taking from her, and not a lot of people were giving it back. Well, I suppose Miles was in his way… maybe he gave back a little."

"How?" Charlie asked.

I looked at the kid. "Next question."

Then his cheeks started to blush. Okay, so the kid was sharp.

"So for Gold. How do we do this? How do we figure out that he did it, and how do we prove it? Can we prove it?" Then Bella looked out the window that faced out onto 7th. She got that way when she thought, staring out at things. Then she looked back at me. "So what did he have to gain?"

I didn't know what he had to gain, that was the problem. "I think he was just mad. That night when she was throwing everybody out of her life, she told him she was changing the contract or walking out. And by the way, Dante was helping her redo the contract."

"What do you mean, change the contract?"

"Well, from what I hear, he had a contract that pretty much gave him everything she made for the studio. And she got a little. Pretty bad for a top star. Basically, he owned her."

"But the magazines said she was making millions?"

"She did. For him. And near as I can tell, everyone else had their hands in her pockets. And she was done with it."

It slowly started to sink in through the haze of sleep deprivation, Liliana really was like the golden goose. And everyone wanted to eat her for Sunday lunch. I can see how she got to where she did that night, telling everybody where they could get off.

"So no one had a reason for her to die, really. Nobody would want her to die, otherwise the gravy train ended."

I nodded at Bella. "That's about the size of it. And that's what doesn't make complete sense."

Charlie looked up from his pad that he hadn't written a word down on. "Then why would Gold want to kill her?"

I looked at Charlie, then at them both. "I figure it was anger. Someone tries to leave your shop? And you don't want them to? Maybe he just snapped. Dante said Gold was having some money problems."

Bella looked at me, or at least half into me. The rest of her was focused someplace else in her mind, thinking. "Then it makes no sense for him to kill her. At all. There had to have been something…" Then she looked straight into my eyes like she understood something. Then ran out to the outer office.

I looked at Charlie. He looked back at me, and we both shrugged.

Bella came back into my office with a stack of magazines in her hands.

Her Hollywood fan magazines.

I stared at them. "You have enough of 'em."

Bella looked at me, her red lipsticked lips getting a little on the thin side. Not very happy with me. "Look, I work hard — when there's things to do. But if you don't give me anything to do, and keep it all to yourself — for some unknown, ungodly reason — just what in the hell am I supposed to do? Sit and twiddle my thumbs waiting until you actually let me *do* something?"

This had gotten a little off track. "Point taken."

"Humph." She said it like she had just scored a point of some kind. And she had. "Now…" She handed Charlie half the stack. "Look in there for an article on Katie Wilder."

Charlie looked at her. "The dancer?"

"Yes," Bella said. She rifled quickly through one magazine from her own pile, finished it, then slapped it down on top of my desk and started into the next. "I know it's in here…"

Charlie looked through a few of his as Bella looked through hers, then held one up, opened to the first few pages. "Is this it?"

Bella looked at the rag. "Yes." And took it from Charlie and held it up for me. On the page was a photograph of Katie Wilder, made up like some dancehall girl from the wild west, complete with a garter on a leg and a million-dollar smile.

Then Bella pulled the magazine back to the desk and traced her finger down the article until she found what she was looking for. "Here," she tapped the magazine, "The studio has her legs insured for one million dollars."

Charlie looked at her. "One million dollars?"

I frowned. "That's just publicity."

Bella shook her head. "No, it's real. A friend of mine who works over at the insurance agency that handled it said it was." She slapped the rag down onto the desk. "Is that enough to kill Liliana over?"

I had to admit, that was powerful motivation for anyone to do something over. If Liliana was insured. And especially if she was going to leave anyway. "How do we know if there was one? That he had a policy on her? And what would it be, on her life?"

Bella's mind started working and she looked back out the window. "I could call my friend, see if they have anything. But there are a lot of insurance agencies in town."

"Big enough to handle that large a policy?"

"Probably. Not to mention New York."

I hadn't even thought of that. Bella was good. "Can you call your friend at least?"

"Sure. And I'll ask her to ask around the other agencies."

"There you're talking."

Charlie spoke up. "But is that going to be enough for a judge?"

He was right. That a policy existed didn't prove Gold did it. Or how. Or... anything. But — I got up and turned around to grab my jacket, not even sure what I was going to do. The sleep was still there at the edges of my head, but I had to do something. At least there was something now that I could do.

Bella looked confused. "Where are you going?"

Sometimes the only thing you can do is whatever you can do.

I knew running off to the studio with some half-baked, half-cocked idea was stupid. But sometimes you just have to shake the world a little to get things to turn your way. It was an old Marine trick I learned — never stand still. You *always* make something happen. You have to. Otherwise, you're dead.

And I wasn't letting Miles' mother down.

That woman had somehow burrowed her way straight into my head. She was a persistent thing. An against all the odds. Against the entire world.

That was a Marine, too. You got things done.

No matter what.

Until you died.

I looked at Bella. "I'm going to the studio to see if I can find the policy myself."

Her jaw dropped.

Charlie's did, too. "How are you going to do that?"

I shrugged my shoulders as I buttoned my jacket. "I don't know."

I did, but it was too crazy. I was going off half-cocked, and half out of my mind and for an ex-Marine, that was about status quo.

I left the office and headed to the studio.

Like a bull headed for a china shop.

Chapter 33

I KEEP A PAIR of used coveralls in my car at all times. It's not that I don't mind getting myself dirty occasionally. For the first sixteen years of my life, that's all I lived in on the farm. But now I like to keep them around for other things.

I parked a couple streets down from the studio, slipped into my coveralls, and grabbed the universal symbol of *you need help* — a plunger. I slung the plunger over my shoulder and headed toward the studio.

I was still out of it from no sleep, or finally getting some, as I walked down the sidewalk toward the main gate. It was as if I was having the happiest day of my life, and I swore, I probably had a smile on my mug. Not because I was happy, but because I didn't know where the hell I was. What I was about to do.

Oh, I knew what I was about to do, and I didn't care. And that was the problem.

My plan was to walk up to the gate and bluff my way through with my coveralls, but as luck would have it, I didn't need to do that. Ahead, and tying up the gate and guard, was a large delivery truck. Edward's Produce, if the painting on the side of it was to be believed. And I guess I believed it.

The guard shack was on the other side of the truck and I just walked onto the lot right as the truck pulled forward. I didn't even have to break my stride and I just kept going. And I felt like whistling.

"Hey you!"

That didn't sound right, because in my delirious mind everything was going to work out okay. Happy endings all around, right?

After all, it was a movie studio. Things always worked out great.

"You, in the coveralls — halt!"

No… I didn't like the sound of that at all.

I turned around to face the burly guard walking straight toward me, his hand on his hip, or more accurately, on the billy club that rested there. He made a beeline for me, his eyes focused on me like black beads.

Apparently he didn't want to yell anymore because he waited until he got right in front of my face, letting me know exactly who's boss. "Next time, use the back gate."

"Yes sir, no problem at all." I saluted him with my free hand and I couldn't believe it. Maybe things were starting to break for me. And for Miles' mom. "I've been working all night and I'm a little out of my mind."

The guard just stared at me for an extra couple of seconds, then walked back to his line of cars. And I turned and got myself out of his sight.

Well… that went according to plan.

I made a beeline for the large office building to my right. It looked like a smaller version of the administration building on the other side of the lot where Gold had his office. Just as I got to the brown wooden door, it opened, and Stan, Gold's security guy, walked out.

I did a quick about face and hunched over while walking away from the place and hoped he didn't see me.

I kept myself low, kept the business end of the plunger next to my face, and put a little hitch in my step just to keep things confusing. I ducked around the corner of the building and out of sight. At least I hoped out of sight.

I heard nothing from behind. No Stan calling my name or, worse, pulling a gun on me. So I figured the coast was clear.

Just so there were no surprises, I walked back over to the side of the building, popped my head out, and watched as Stan kept walking toward the other side of the lot, and most likely, back to Gold.

I wondered what he was doing in the building, but I suppose as head of security he could do whatever he wanted.

A dame in a red dress walked past on the sidewalk, staring at me looking around the corner. I smiled. "Playing hide and seek."

She didn't smile back.

I decided to get on with what I came there to do. With Stan gone and specifically gone out of this building, I poked around and found a back door in and, as quickly as I could, got myself into a men's room.

It was small, with white tiles on the floor, two stalls and one urinal, and I set down the plunger in the corner and got about taking my coveralls off, and down to my rather rumpled suit. It would have to do.

I looked at the coveralls in my hand and the plunger in the corner. Neither one of them were expensive, but they weren't free either. I would come back for them after I was done. It was the small things that mattered when you lived during a Depression.

I looked down at my shoes and they were scuffed. Gold would definitely not approve.

The hell with him.

I got out of there and got on to the next step of my suicide plan.

Chapter 34

I HAD TO FIND the offices where insurance documents were taken care of, so hoped my luck from the guard at the main gate would hold out.

I was on the sidewalk, in back of the building I'd just lost my coveralls in.

I faced into a small square park tucked in the back there that was green and shaded, pink flowers along the edges, with a bench in front of me on the one side, and another bench on the other side. A little piece of paradise, tucked away in the middle of a magic factory.

A girl, probably a secretary, sat on the bench in front of me smoking and, like any lost tourist looking for an insurance office, I decided to ask a local. "Hi, sorry to bother you…"

She turned. She wore a simple white dress with a small pattern of blue and yellow flowers on it, a small white lace collar at her neck, and a smile above that, directed at me. And I swore she winked. "No bother at all. Like to have a seat?"

This day was getting more interesting.

I looked down and she had one creamy white leg draped over

the other, a small brown shoe dangling off her foot, the strap undone, and me heading toward coming undone in front of her. I collected myself and focused. "Actually," I flashed open my coat jacket just a little, but not too much that she could see anything. "I have some insurance papers I have to deliver. But you know me… when I left the office my secretary told me where to go, but I've forgotten already." I finished it with a smile.

She kept up her smile at me, with a little hint of something fun at the edges. "That's just the point, though, isn't it? I don't know you. So why don't you sit here next to me, and we can remedy that." She finished off by bouncing her foot up and down just enough so that her shoe threatened to come all the way off.

Hmm… A dame finally gets interested in me, but I'm on a case. Trying to save a guy. It's called bad timing for a reason. "Believe me, you don't know how much I'd like you to get to know me, but if I don't get this done, someone's gonna die."

The girl laughed. "Well, we wouldn't want that now, would we?" Her laugh dropped back down to a smile, and if I wasn't mistaken, dropped into some kind of regret shadowing on her face.

I hoped mine was showing through on my own.

She took a small breath and plunged on. "So, where do you need to go?"

It didn't take long, and as it turned out, the offices were in the building I had just come out of, up on the third floor. Which was good. I would be well away from Gold.

From the time I turned from the girl until the time I got up to the third floor of the building, I'd come up with my plan. It was a stupid plan. It was an asinine plan. But that's what you get when you don't sleep.

I walked down the third floor corridor, a number of glass doors on either side of the hall holding all the efficient office workers inside. Well, that was about to change.

At the end of the corridor I found the office I needed, the one that handled all insurance paperwork for the studio, presided over, the door told me, by one Lawrence Rock.

I walked back to the other end of the corridor, turned back to face the emptiness and closed doors of the thirty offices in front of me, pulled in a good slug of air, opened my mouth, and yelled. "Fire!"

I started with the door to my left and banged on it like I meant to kill everyone inside. "Fire!"

Now, the funny thing is, when somebody hears fire, the first thing they think is, this can't be happening. But when you have a crazy, six-foot guy, completely disheveled and shouting into your face, into your office, the second thing you do, and you do it pretty quickly, is get your backside up and run for an exit as fast as you can.

And… my plan worked like a charm.

By the time I made it halfway down the hall, most of the office doors had been slammed open and the corridor was now crowded with people heading for the stairs at either end of the long corridor.

Me? I pushed my way through the oncoming traffic until I finally made it back to the insurance door, and walked inside.

And inside, the place was empty. At least of people.

It was an office full of file cabinets, which is what I expected. Which is what I had hoped. File cabinets meant a lot of paper, and a lot of paper filed neat and clean.

I figured I had probably three minutes, maybe five minutes tops, before somebody found me up here. By that time, hopefully there was enough confusion down below that I could slip out. If I found what I was looking for. If I even knew what I was looking for. Some kind of insurance document that said that Gold had insured Liliana for a lot of money.

It was crazy. But it's all we had.

I had some vague hope that any insurance policies would be filed in a file marked Liliana McGann. I'm kind of simple that way.

I counted eighteen file cabinets lining the walls of the main office I was in, with another frosted door to the back, with Larry's name stenciled on it.

I found the filing cabinet with McA through McM on it, pulled it open, and searched for Liliana's name — McGann.

And there was nothing. No McGann anywhere. Not that I expected there to be. I'd already gotten lucky with the guard and the girl… what were the chances of three nice things happening in a row?

If the rest of my life was any indication, the odds were zero.

I thought of looking by movie title, but I only remembered one of her movies, and that one wasn't that good. Then something hit me. If Liliana was the top star on the lot, why would she be kept in the regular files? She probably wouldn't. Then I thought that maybe all her files were kept in Gold's office. And my heart sank.

Nothing I could do about it. So I kept focused on what was right in front of me. Finish the job I came here to do.

Then I saw that frosted glass door into Larry's office again, and I wondered.

I yanked open the frosted glass door and the office inside was a large office, maybe twenty by twenty. I hit the jackpot because in the corner was a safe. A very common, Washington D7 safe.

I kept one of those down in the basement at my office, mostly because it wasn't a challenge anymore. It was a three-tumbler safe, and I could crack one of those in my sleep. Whether I could do it in three minutes we'd have to see.

The rest of the office held a few other filing cabinets, a large desk tucked into the corner, a few pictures of family on the desk, and a couple of pictures up on the wall with Louis Gold and a bald headed guy I assume was Larry himself. They looked chummy.

On the wall opposite the windows that looked out onto the studio below, another frosted glass door stood closed that lead back out into the corridor. A nice escape route for old Larry. If he didn't want to see anyone come a-calling.

I figured what I was looking for was not going to be in any of the filing cabinets, so I got myself over to the safe and down on one knee.

The D7 was big, black, and had a three-pack combination,

meaning there were three disks inside the mechanism, which meant three numbers you needed to discover. Each time you got a number, one disc inside aligned with a small v-notch facing up, which, when you got all three notches facing up, allowed the thin bar of the locking mechanism to fall into place and out of the way of the lock. Bingo — you had an open safe. Easy.

For me.

Except for the amount of time.

Everything was silent from out in the corridor, until it wasn't. I heard two sets of shoes running up the corridor, and off in the distance was the shrill sound of a siren.

First one shadow passed the door out into the corridor, then another. And I heard a couple of muffled words passing between the two. I wasn't sure what they said, but I hoped it was that they were on their way down the stairs outside.

I focused on the safe and tried to get that thing open.

I felt one tumbler catch, and then fall into place as the muffled voices became a little less muffled — as they entered Larry's outer office.

I could have kicked myself that I didn't shut the door into Larry's office where I now stood next to a safe trying to crack it.

I should leave… just leave.

Instead I focused inside myself, and then focused on the lock. Only two more numbers left.

And that's when the guys walked into Larry's office, seeing me, yeah, squatting next to the safe.

I smiled up at them with my best innocent smile.

They were smaller guys, as guys went, both shorter than me, both in blue studio guard uniforms. And both crowded together in the doorway, I think not quite believing what they saw. Shocked pretty much described it. I guess they were only looking for a fire.

And shocked pretty much described it for me, too, on account of I didn't exactly want them to be there.

"Who the hell are you?" That was from the short guard on the left. According to his name tag, his name was Miles. I found that kind of funny.

I stood up a little shaky on my legs — it seemed like every-thing was going to hell in my body — and I gave them the best soap-selling smile I could muster. "Larry there called me because he forgot his combination. I was just helping him out." And I kept up the smile like I meant it.

They didn't smile.

And they meant it.

They split apart, one moving slowly to the left while the other drifted to the right, trying to box me in. I only had one hope, Larry's not-so-secret back door. And I ran for it.

The two guys rushed after me and I grabbed a coat rack and two chairs, tossing them back in front of them. The guard from the left caught a chair and took a dive, hitting the floor like a sack of potatoes. The guard from the right just got his hand on my shoulder, then I wheeled around with my elbow and caught him square in the face.

It hit him hard and my elbow went numb, but the way I cracked him, he went down more than numb. He went down — out.

I rushed out Larry's back door and out into the corridor.

There were a couple of other guys down at the other end. But ones I didn't want to see. The two bald goons from Gold's office. They recognized me. And they didn't speak a word. They didn't have to. They just pulled their guns. And I got the hell out of there.

I took the stairs next to Larry's office and I took them five at a time, all the way down until I hit the first floor, then I rushed out the door to the outside.

Chapter 35

AS I RAN OUT the door, trying to slow down enough not to call attention to myself, a ring of people were scattered around the outside of the building. All milling around, wondering where the fire was.

And, I suppose, enjoying a little break in the Southern California sun.

I headed up a sidewalk away from the building and deeper into the studio lot.

As I saw in my first visit, the roads that cut around the place were narrow and long. I got myself off onto a couple of the smaller streets leading away from the main street I had come up on, and found myself in the middle of a distinctly downtown street. Probably fresh out of somebody's idea of what New York looked like.

I wondered if it was the New York that Gold remembered. But with how clean and tidy everything was, my guess was that this was nothing like what Gold knew. This was a fairytale version of the place.

And it had a decidedly smaller feel to it. There were small store fronts to my left and right that then led into what looked like a bunch of brownstone buildings, complete with stoops out front.

Everything was clean and tidy, and there was not a person on the street. A little odd, and truth be told, scary for me. I liked a few more people around me. Made me think I wasn't alone.

Then I heard footsteps behind me. I guess I got my wish. Damn it.

I ran straight for another block until I cleared the brownstones, then made a left onto one of the avenues, Avenue N.

There were cars and trucks tucked against the right side of the avenue, the left clear to allow any equipment to shuttle between the large barn-like studio buildings on either side.

A little further down, on a soundstage with a large white *31* painted on the corner of it, a ramp led up to my right and to a door that unfortunately had a red light blazing over the top of it.

Somebody was making a movie inside.

Not a good place to go, I decided, and continued running ahead until I saw a small road to the right, which I took.

Then right after that I took a left into a small alleyway, where a number of doorways entered tall buildings on either side of me. There were a series of windows at ground level, and nothing above that but large, faceless walls that seemed to block out the sun from above.

I heard shouting in back of me and figured the best thing I could do would be to get inside one of the buildings. I picked the building to my right and walked in through the cream-colored nondescript door with *25-7* written on it.

Inside, a small staircase ahead of me headed straight up to the second floor, while a long corridor headed left and right of me. I didn't hear voices outside, but the quicker I got inside some other door, the better I would be.

So I immediately headed down the corridor to my left.

There were doors on either side of the corridor. The ones to the left would have windows that faced outside and onto the small alleyway that I had just come down, so I picked a random door on the right, hoping for nothing on the other side but silence and peace. The door had *3E* stenciled on it, so I opened it and went inside.

Into a junk shop.

Bicycle tires, pots and pans, brass lamps, and golf clubs lined the walls, with stuffed pheasants, a stuffed sheep standing on the floor, and honest to God, a stuffed horse head attached to the wall in front of me and staring me right in the eye.

"You from *Wings Over Man?*"

The voice was spoken over the small, whining sound of an electrical motor, and came from my right. I looked over to a young guy, maybe only eighteen. He had long brown hair, with a small jeweler's magnifying piece stuck over his right eye, and he stood behind a small counter that led into what looked like a giant, dimly lit storeroom that trailed off in back of him.

And he was painfully thin.

He kept looking at me because I didn't answer him. I guess the horse head had thrown me off. "Are you from *Wings Over Man?*"

I looked to either side of him, and the walls of the place, besides the odd pieces of junk, were covered also in movie posters. *Wings Over Man* must be a movie. Being shot. I was in a studio. My detecting skills were amazing me at the moment. "Yeah… from *Wings Over Man.*"

The young guy smiled. "Good, I'm almost finished."

The guy sat back down behind his counter that came up to my belt. I walked over and looked. In his hand, the thing making the high-pitched whine, was some kind of thing that looked like a dentist's drill.

He didn't even look up at me and kept on working, but kept up a conversation like he'd known me forever. "There's some coffee over there if you want it. It's a long run from studio 48, huh?"

I looked over, and sure enough, there was a hot plate with a coffeepot on it, next to an armadillo. And a suit of armor.

I grabbed a mug from next to the armadillo and poured myself a cup. I think I could like this place.

The whining didn't let up, and I wondered if he was tattooing the Gettysburg Address on a whale tooth or something. Who knows what kind of movies got made here. "How's it coming over there?"

"Oh…" I took a sip of the coffee. It was actually good. "You know how it is, slow some days, then they're clawing at your butt the next."

"Amen to that." The young guy finished up what he was doing, picked up a small, golden metal object, and blew onto it in front of him. He held it up to a light, inspecting it, then nodded his head. "I think this should do it."

He reached his hand out across the counter to me, offering the object.

It was a small lighter.

And my heart leapt into my throat. It was engraved, with two initials, *A* and *G*, a circle containing the two letters. It was a simple circle, a line, no flourishes, but the ghost of another golden lighter danced in front of my eyes.

I took it in my hand.

It was still warm from his touch.

"It was a rush job." The guy smiled at me. His eyes were set wide apart and were brown. And his smile was genuine, "But I did the best I could do."

"It…" I looked back down at it, amazed. "Looks good."

He sat back down in his seat behind the counter and started to brush small bits of metal dust from the top of the desk he worked at.

I wondered if my luck was starting to change. "Hey, if we needed it, how hard would it be to make that circle around the letter into something a little more fancy… like scrollwork?"

The young guy looked up at me, a question on his face. "That would be easy. I can do that in my sleep."

I saw a piece of paper to the side on his desk and I reached over for it, along with a pencil that sat next to it. I drew a circle with curly scrollwork on it, at least something that looked like it might be what was on the lighter found next to Liliana. Then I put an *M* in the middle of it and showed the drawing to the guy. "Do you think you could do something like this?"

The kid looked up at me, a question in his eyes. "Yeah… Why are you looking?"

I took a leap. "A special project for Mr. Gold." I hoped I wasn't spilling anything too quickly here.

"That's kind of funny, Mr. Gold needed one of these last year. He need another one now?"

I kept myself cool. "Right, I forgot about that one. Well, this one is to replace that one. Say, when did you make that other one?"

The kid picked up a sandwich lying at the far corner of his desk. A baloney one from the looks of it. Then he took a bite out of it like he hadn't eaten in forever. "It was last summer." He took another bite.

My heart raced. "You don't remember exactly when, do you?"

The guy laughed. "Course I do. He kept me late on a Friday to do it. I was due to go up to Lake Arrowhead that night. Got myself a place up there."

I looked at the kid and didn't think he had that much money.

The kid smiled, understanding. He took another bite of his sandwich, a little piece of bread falling down from the corner of his mouth. "It's my uncle's. But I'm hoping it's mine. At least one day, on account of he doesn't have any kids." The kid smiled.

A very smart kid. "Do you remember the date?"

"Sure thing, July third. My uncle and I were going to barbecue that next day. The Fourth of July."

"And that's when Mr. Gold came in to get this?"

The kid laughed. "Mr. Gold doesn't do anything. His head of security came over, I never remember his name."

"Stan," I offered.

The guy nodded. "Yeah, Stan. Which I thought was kind of strange. He has nothing to do with any of the pictures. But when the old man asks, you do whatever is needed." The kid wiped his face with his hand, then just as quickly stuffed the rest of the sandwich back into it. He was enjoying himself.

Meanwhile, I was, too. That Friday, July third, was the night Liliana went out for her dinner and was killed.

The kid had engraved the lighter, at the request of Gold. This was what was called in the business a smoking gun. And I had him.

"Say, you're not going anywhere tonight, are you?"

"Nope. Working late. Got your picture and that horse one."

I wondered if they'd need a horse's head for it. But either way, the kid was sticking, and I had to call Cardon. He'd have to pick up the kid, ask him a few questions, and then give the judge a call. And of course, arrest Gold. It was all too perfect. And I loved it.

A wall clock behind the kid said it was 5:18 p.m. on the dot. Plenty of time. I reached across the counter and offered my hand. "My name is John."

The kid shifted his sandwich from his right hand into his left, then stuck his right hand out and pumped mine like a guy who meant it. "George Standish. At your service. Assistant prop master for Golden Pictures." The kid looked around the counter and the massive warehouse behind him, filled as far as I could see with shelves stacked with every other piece of junk you could imagine under the sun. He laughed. "Who would've thunk all of this stuff is a job? I guess I'm lucky I got a job at all."

"Yeah, luck… I was thinking the exact same thing."

A phone sat on the corner of George's desk but I didn't dare use it. I didn't want to scare the kid. Or have him asking any questions before I had Cardon right here. I would duck into one of the other offices nearby and sweet talk myself into a phone.

George reached over for a small group of papers on his desk and set them up on the counter in front of me. "You'll need to sign for the lighter."

"Oh, right…"

He pointed to a small slip of paper with a signature line on it. It was attached to a larger piece of paper complete with a couple of names, the name of the movie, and a rough drawing of the *A* and *G* inside the circle. Then George handed me a pen.

I felt guilty. I didn't exactly want to take the lighter. Somebody was going to be very angry—

The door behind me into the small room opened. I hoped it wasn't the real person looking for the lighter. It wasn't. It was Gold's two goons.

They saw me.

And ran at me.

Chapter 36

I STOOD THERE BETWEEN Gold's two goons rushing toward me and the young guy who was Miles' salvation behind me.

If I pulled my guns, then there was a good chance they would pull theirs and an even better chance that young George would end up dead. Not to mention me, too.

And there was no way I was going to be able to take George with me, so I did the next best thing: I turned around and dove straight over the counter, my size twelve shoes heading straight toward George's face. Now there was nothing mean at all in that move, just the sincere desire that he would react like 99 percent of all humans on the face of the Earth, and dive.

And he did. Like a champ.

George hit the floor with a flop, while I tucked, rolled, and was up and dashing into the warehouse beyond like a sprinter trying to be a cheetah.

At least I knew George was out of the way of any danger, and I could call Cardon and get him over here quick.

I found myself in a very large warehouse, shelves stacked to the ceiling from one wall to the other. The row I headed down looked like it stretched at least over two hundred feet back. But being essentially a long aisle back, it was also the perfect thing to be shooting down. A fish in a barrel. So like the studio streets outside, I started taking quick lefts and rights down the cross rows, trying to get as far back into the place as I could get and then figure out what I was going to do.

With every shelf that I passed, I began to see a method to the madness.

Each shelf contained letters and numbers to, I guess, form some kind of filing system. And on all the shelves? The entire recorded history of man's junk.

There was everything you can imagine. There were golf clubs lying on the shelves, radios, and old things that look like from the 1800s.

Groups of dishes sat on one shelf I passed, with groups of tools on another.

I heard the two goons somewhere behind me as I cut from one row over to another, all the while steadily heading toward the back of the warehouse. Hopefully as far as I could get away from them.

As I ran, I ran past junk from Japan, then junk from Italy, past household things from the 1700s, then right past what looked like the complete contents of the library of Cornelius Vanderbilt himself.

Everything looked like it had some kind of place, all of it with the letters and numbers on every shelf there. Apparently George or his boss was very, very organized.

As I flew along, all in all the place smelled like dust and dry air, mold, and things falling apart. Like any good grandfather's attic, and I could see why George liked it there so much.

I hoped he could keep his job after he testified against Gold.

A single gunshot rang out and what looked like a Ming vase to my left shattered. I took a quick left and found myself in the final aisle that followed the wall straight to the back corner of the place. And I was out of options.

There had to be a door.

Right?

As I got closer and closer to the end of the aisle, and the farthest point I could run, the junk started to run up in time — from the 1600s, to the 1700s, and finally to what looked like the old wild west of the 1800s.

And that's when I saw the door.

Cut neatly into the back wall of the place, surrounded on all sides by shelves, I ran straight at it and planted a size twelve shoe right next to a big old padlock, hoping that the whole door itself would wrench right away from the wall.

It didn't. And I bounced.

Right off the damn thing and onto my backside.

Just as two shots drilled themselves in the middle of the door. Okay, a little more luck there.

I looked back at one goon running straight at me, his gun leveled, then I pulled out both of mine and let fly with six quick shots, all aimed a little above his head. I wasn't trying to kill the guy, even though he was trying to do that exact thing to me.

I guess I have a conscience.

The goon dropped fast, getting caught in his own feet, and he pitched forward and slammed his face right down on the concrete floor. I took that opportunity to turn back to the door and pumped another six shots into the padlock holding the door locked.

This time the thing gave as I planted my shoe right into it, the door snapping open to a beautiful sunshiny day on the other side. I ran out and onto a residential street that butted up to the back of the studio, then ran.

I did my same left and right routine down alleys and across yards of the neighborhood until I knew nobody had followed me. I had beaten them.

Then I headed to my car as fast as I could.

I'd make the call from my office, and Cardon would be back fast to get George.

And then I was going to officially take a three-day nap.

Done.

***

George was worried when he heard all the shots from back in the warehouse and got on the phone to studio security.

Then in the middle of telling the operator on the other side, "…yeah, two big guys, and a guy from *Wings Over*—" the line went dead.

George looked down at the phone, and a large finger held the cradle crushed down.

George looked up, and one of the two big bald guys that had walked in and had started chasing the first guy stood next to George. Then the other walked up, his brown eyes cutting into George.

And suddenly George started to not feel good about this.

The taller guy with his finger on the cradle of the phone smiled. "What did you two talk about?"

And the guy's smile turned to a sneer.

And George suddenly felt even beyond not good about this. And as stupid as it sounded, he wanted his mother.

Chapter 37

SOMETHING WAS WRONG, AND I didn't know what it was.

I sat in my office and couldn't do a damn thing. I'd gotten to the office fast after leaving the studio, and called Cardon at his office — at the diner. It was afternoon. Of course he was there. I told him about George and the engraving, and he went over to take a look and promised to call me back as soon as he got him.

That was an hour and half ago.

Already it was seven o'clock, and getting way too close to midnight for me. And, I'm sure, for Miles.

I pushed up from behind my desk and walked over to the window out on 7th. It was evening already, the dark had fallen, and the traffic was flowing toward the west. Out and away from downtown.

I wasn't going to be able to sleep until this was all over. Either way.

The phone rang and I dove for it at my desk. "Hello?"

"Devin, this is Cardon. It's a no go. The kid wasn't there."

"*What*? What do you mean he wasn't there?"

"I mean he wasn't there."

"You went to the props department, right?"

"Yes. The horsehead and all. The kid wasn't there."

"Maybe he was at dinner or something, did you check the cafeteria?"

"They call it the commissary, and no, he wasn't there, either."

"Then someplace else. You gotta find him, Cardon."

"They told me he had left work early."

My heart sank. "Early? He was staying there for a couple of movies that were being shot."

"He was sick. Supposedly. Look, Devin, I only know what they told me."

"Who told you?"

Bella came in from the outer office, Charlie right behind her. Neither one of them looked happy.

I heard a piece of paper flip on the other end of the line, then I caught the sounds of traffic beyond that. "A guy named Brown. He's in security there."

I didn't know a guy named Brown, maybe it was one of the goons. "Was he big?"

"No. Medium size."

"Pasty white skin, looks nasty?"

"That's him."

"Stan. Gold's head of security."

"That's the name."

This I didn't like. What was Stan doing… that was a stupid question. They'd gotten George, and my heart really sank then.

Everything was gone for Miles. Unless we could find George. And judging from the traffic noise coming from Cardon's end of the line, he wasn't at the studio anymore. "You in a phone booth?"

"Yeah. I didn't want to use the phone there."

Everything was gone. "Did you go to the back of the props warehouse? Did you find the door at least? There should have been at least three slugs in it."

"I checked it. It looked new."

"What you mean new?"

182

"Look Devin, I checked the door and it was new."

"I don't suppose there was a padlock on it with six bullet holes in it?"

"No padlock. Just the door. All new and freshly painted. Which leaves me a little questioning right now, to be honest. The kid is missing, and the door is completely new. I'm not dumb as a detective."

"I didn't say you were." At least Cardon was believing me. But I didn't know what to do next.

"They gave me his home address, and his license plate number. I'm heading over to check there right now."

George wasn't going to be there, and I knew it in my bones. "Look, Cardon, I don't have a good feeling about this. Can you check around the lot a little more?"

"I'm already gone. And what do you want, me to check every single building on the lot? That'd take days. I have a lead and I'm going to follow it. That is, if you'll stop talking."

I looked up at the clock — 7:49 p.m. — and Miles had about four hours left. And we had nothing. Unless Cardon could find George, and I had less and less of an idea that he would. I couldn't believe I talked to the kid and didn't try to take him out of there. And now he was dead. Or at least that's where my mind went.

"Devin, I've got to get going."

"Okay, but check back in here every thirty minutes if you can. I'll have Bella stay here on the phone, and we can coordinate. I have a few ideas."

"What ideas?"

I wasn't sure, but they probably involved going back to the studio. "I don't know yet. But Cardon, please, whatever you do, keep calling back in here and we'll get it figured out. Just… we need something, Cardon."

"I know. You said the judge would be at Toots' tonight?"

"Yeah."

"All night?"

"I'll make sure of it."

"Gotta go." And Cardon clicked off on the other end.
I had to go, too.
For anything I could find.

Chapter 38

AS SOON AS I hung up the phone, Bella was on me. "What happened?"

I took the two shoulder holsters off the coat rack behind my desk and slung them on. "Nothing. Except the kid wasn't there."

"What do you mean wasn't there?"

I checked my two guns, then took my jacket off the coat rack and slung that over everything else. "I think they got him. Cardon is going to check at the kid's house. They say he left early, but I don't think so. Gold's head of security was giving Cardon the tour."

"Why him?"

I looked at Bella. "Exactly." Then I headed for the outer office. "Give Toots a call and tell him to make sure the judge doesn't leave. Ever. Until we call there… or I guess if midnight hits."

"Did you give Cardon the number there?"

I had forgotten. "No."

Bella looked at me like she couldn't let me do anything. "I'll make sure he has it."

"What can I do?" Charlie asked.

I looked at him. "At this point, nothing."

If I wasn't mistaken, Charlie looked a little angry. I hoped not at me. "Just… stay here. There may be something, who knows. Just… stay here."

Charlie nodded.

I pulled the outer door open with a jerk, just as a girl tried walking in.

The girl — was June.

Secretary to Horace P. Streck, Attorney at Law.

I almost hit her, her blue eyes in shock and her short blonde hair just peeking out from under a small, conservative black hat.

June took a step back in shock, but then held her ground looking up at me. "Can I come in?"

I wasn't sure why she was there. Unless Streck had had a change of heart and sent over the rest of the file. I had my doubts. "Of course. Come on in."

The girl looked past me as Bella and Charlie walked out of my office and into the outer office. It was starting to get cozy.

Bella had the same questioning look in her eyes as I did, but she motioned to June. "Would you like some coffee?" Bella already headed to the hot plate and the pot on top of it.

"No. I just wanted to…" June looked at all three of us, paying particular attention to Charlie, for some reason. He was taller than her, and I wondered if maybe they went to school together or something. That is, until Charlie's father kicked him out and he had to become an adult.

"Please, have a seat at least." Bella was trying to make the girl feel welcome at least.

"I don't have too long," June began, "I have to get back to my boy." Then she reached into the small black purse she held in a nervous hand and pulled out a small white envelope and held it out to me.

I looked at the small girl and the small envelope. Then I took it from her.

There was still the gun-shyness to her, and I hated Streck for putting that into her. But for some reason, as the envelope left her hand, June looked like there was a small bit of something else coming into her. And if I wasn't mistaken, it looked like victory. "It came in one day at the office. Soon after Mr. Streck got the White case."

I turned the envelope over and it was addressed to "Miles White's Lawyer," with no return address. The writing was loopy, like it was written by a young girl, and the envelope was stamped September of last year.

I opened it. It was a two page letter, written in the same girl's handwriting as the address.

And I read it.

It told of how the girl who wrote the letter had run away from home and had planned to hitchhike to San Francisco. She was picked up along the way by a woman in a car who took her as far as Hollywood. The woman listened to the girl's story, that she was running from home, and related to it. The woman had wanted to run away from home herself when she was young, but her mother had caught her and kept her there. The woman had started acting when she was a kid, and the mother knew a good thing when she saw it.

The woman was Liliana McGann.

When they pulled up to Liliana's restaurant, as far as Liliana was going to go, the letter said a car was waiting in the shadows.

Liliana gave the girl ten dollars to help her out and told her if she didn't make it to San Francisco, or ended up wanting to stay, the girl should come back and Liliana would find her a job in the restaurant.

The girl headed out to the street as Liliana headed over to the car. Liliana seemed to know who was inside.

The girl got to the street, but as soon as she did, something didn't feel right. So she snuck back toward the courtyard.

The girl watched the car for a bit and saw a lot of movement inside, then a couple of minutes later the driver and an older, larger man got out of the back of the car. They carried Liliana into the restaurant by the feet and shoulders. She looked like she was knocked out cold.

The girl went up to a window when they were inside the restaurant, but then got scared and ran. And that was that. The letter said she didn't think either of the two men looked like Miles White.

So she sent the letter to the lawyer… she didn't trust the cops.

I looked up at June. "Did you read this?"

She nodded.

"Did Streck talk with the girl?"

June shook her head. "He didn't even look for her."

"What is it?" Bella asked.

"An eyewitness. Said a car was there waiting for Liliana when she got back to the restaurant that night." I turned back to June. "Why didn't he look? He was defending Miles." I couldn't believe it. "He read it, right?"

"Yes. I gave it to him the day it arrived in the mail. Then later that night, I was emptying his trash bin and found it there."

Bella looked at June. "He threw it away?" She took the letter.

"I don't know why I kept it," June said, "But I guess for this."

Bella held the second page of the letter up to me and pointed to a group of numbers and letters at the bottom. "Is that what I think it is?"

I wasn't looking at her, but I knew what she was pointing at. "A license plate number." I was already thinking what it meant.

Charlie got excited. "Then we have him. Or whoever it was."

"I don't think so…"

Charlie looked at me. "Why?"

Bella answered. "Because without the girl to confirm the story, the letter is meaningless."

"But," Charlie started, "it has to count for something."

"It does." I took a deep breath. "It means we're right, that Miles didn't do it. If we track that license plate number down, I'm sure we'll find it belongs to Gold. Or to Golden Pictures. But without that girl, or the prop guy from the studio… or something that shows absolute proof — we don't have him."

Charlie shook his head. "But you gotta show the letter to that judge."

"I will. As a last resort. But we can't count on it, we need more proof." Then I turned to June. "Thank you for bringing it. But why?"

June looked at Bella. "Something I heard earlier today. And I wanted to do what's right."

Bella smiled at her. "You did."

I looked at June. "If Streck gives you any kind of problem about this, you let me know right away. I'll fix it. Or maybe I'll just go anyway. There were a few things I wanted to talk to him about."

"Don't worry." June looked down. "I'm not going back."

She had a kid. And I knew how much this was costing her.

"I have to get home now." June walked to the door and opened it.

Bella spoke up. "You did do the right thing."

June smiled, barely, and then left.

Chapter 39

I HAD A PROBLEM. Actually, I had a lot of problems.

Cardon was off looking for George in exactly the wrong place. But I didn't know where the right place was. If he was even still alive.

And now with this letter, we had to go out and find a girl.

With only a name, and no address, and no clue how to find her.

Bella reached for the envelope. "What's the return address?"

"There is none." I gave it to her.

Charlie looked over Bella's shoulder at the envelope. "How can there be no return address?"

Then Charlie got quiet.

"Can I see that?"

Bella handed him the envelope.

Charlie looked at the address like he was trying to remember something. Then he looked up at me. "Did she give her name? In the letter?"

I looked down at the bottom of the second page of the letter. "Yeah. Alice Murphy."

Charlie looked like he had seen a ghost. Then he reached out his hand to me, not quite grabbing the letter, but not shying away from it either.

I handed him both pages. "You know her?"

He looked down at the signature on the second page. "Yeah. I know her."

Both Bella and I looked at Charlie at once. Bella beat me to the punch. "Are you kidding?"

Charlie shook his head, I think not believing what he was looking at. "I went to school with her."

That made absolutely no sense. How could we get that lucky?

"How do you know it's her?"

Charlie pointed at the signature. "You see how the *l* in Alice looks like an *o*? And the upper loop in the *h* in Murphy looks like the same *o*? Our eighth grade penmanship teacher used to always yell at her about that." Then he looked up at me. "This is Alice Murphy."

I didn't want to point out to the kid that we already knew it was Alice Murphy. I was just hoping that it was the Alice Murphy he was thinking about. "Do you know where she lives?"

It took only one word from the kid. "Yes."

And we were in business.

Charlie got on the phone to the operator, who put him through to her house; but nobody answered. He tried again and again, and still no answer.

We were running out of time that we didn't have.

"Okay, we don't know when Cardon will be calling back, but he's the best person to go after her. He can talk with her direct."

Charlie spoke up. "But what if he finds the guy from the studio?"

And we still didn't know when, or if, he would check in.

Then something not good started to fill my head. An idea that I didn't like. I tried to push it away, but the more I did, the more it insisted that it was correct. And I thought it was.

The girl was a witness and it seemed like the only one that we were sure of, at least with George out of the picture. But if she couldn't be found, everything was over. We needed everything we could get.

And something kept gnawing at me about the form that George gave me to sign for the lighter. It was a record. And for him, from what I remembered about how everything was organized in that warehouse, my guess was that anything that got made or borrowed from that prop room had a form to keep track of it.

At least I hoped there was a form. Complete with a drawing of an *M* with a circle around it, and the name "Stan" written at the top. At least that was something I could do. Find it.

Between that, finding George, or finding the girl from the letter, something had to pan out for us. And for Miles.

But the only problem was that exactly what I was thinking was what I didn't want to be thinking.

I looked at Charlie. "Do you know how to drive?"

He looked at me, his face a complete question mark. "Why?"

"Bella, give him the keys to your car."

"*What?*"

"You heard me, give him the keys to your car."

"For what?"

I sensed a mutiny coming on. I sighed, "Charlie's going to find the girl."

"*What?*"

Charlie yelped. "Yes! I know I can find her."

"Oh, no you don't. First off, he is not driving my car."

"I can. I swear. I used to drive the old man's car all over the place. When he got drunk, I was the only one who could get him to the speakeasy to get himself another bottle."

Maybe I needed to find Charlie's dad, too. Right after I took care of Streck.

"Did you hear that?" Bella pleaded, trying to make her case. "He only drove to the speakeasy."

I took her by the shoulders since that was the only way we were going to get through this without someone, maybe everyone, being killed. "Bella. I know. You know how to drive, I know you're smart, and I know you'd give it your best shot looking for the girl. But…"

Bella's eyes already started to sink.

"Charlie knows what she looks like. And if she tries to run, where she may try to hide. It's got to be him."

Charlie beamed, and I didn't want him to.

"And I really, and I mean really, need you here on the phone. You're the only one that's going to be able to keep it all coordinated, and if something goes south, and you know it will, I need you to follow through and get this whole thing through. I trust you. And I trust only you to do this."

Bella was mad. As a hornet.

Her mouth twisted into all kinds of shapes as she tried to say all the things she wanted to say, but she kept them to herself. Luckily. "Fine."

"There you go." Then I turned to Charlie and grabbed him by the shoulders. Hard. "And if you so much as take one risk, drive even an ounce over the speed limit, or let anything happen to that girl if you do find her, I will… and I mean *will*… personally kill you."

"And the car," Bella added.

"Goes without saying, Charlie. If you so much as get a scratch on Bella's car, I won't kill you, she will. And that, I can assure you, will be one hell of a lot worse."

And he believed me. I could see it in his eyes. In his bright blue, fifteen-year-old, quaking eyes. "Yes, sir." He turned to Bella. "And ma'am."

She grunted. "I'm no ma'am. Just get my car — and *you* — back here safe."

And she meant it.

Charlie nodded, and Bella handed over the key to her car. Then he headed for the door.

"Charlie." He turned to face me. "You call Bella every time something happens, you understand?"

He nodded his head.

"If you find her, you let Bella know. If you don't find her, you let Bella know. If you run into a problem, you call Bella and let her know. She's the one who will have to coordinate all of us. You got that?"

"Yes."

"Good. Then get going… and good luck."

Charlie opened the door.

"Charlie," Bella began, "Be safe. You understand? You're going to feel all powerful right now, out to save the world, but the first thing is—"

"Be safe. I know." He bowed his head to her and then left.

I looked at Bella and I could see it in her eyes. It was like our first born was going off to war.

And he was. And that's why I was so scared. If anything happened to that kid, I would never forgive myself. He'd grown on me.

And Bella, too.

"He's going to be okay."

Bella looked at me. I'm not sure she believed it.

I stayed just long enough to work out the rest of everything with Bella, then I left, too.

To head back to Golden Pictures.

To hopefully, bring down a king.

Chapter 40

BELLA GOT ON THE phone to Toots. He answered on the second ring.

"Hello!" The sound was loud in the background and Bella could barely hear him over the sound of glasses, and talking, and people having a good time. "Who is it?"

"Toots?"

"Yeah. Who is this?"

"Bella, at Devin's office. You know Judge James?"

There was a slight pause. "Yeah... He's here. You want to talk with him?"

"No. I want you to keep him there."

"Keep him?"

"Yeah, until we give you a call."

Then Bella told him about a complete long shot — to try to save a guy's life.

And she only hoped it would actually work.

Chapter 41

I PULLED UP THE residential street in back of Golden Studios that I had just been running down… not that long ago.

The great hulking masses of the studio buildings on the other side of the street rose up like the faces of mountains. I was only interested in one of the buildings, the one with the shiny new green door on it.

I parked in front of a small bungalow with no lights on inside and headed across the street.

The one thing about Southern California homes, especially in this neighborhood, was that everyone tended to stay inside of them. Which was good for a PI looking to break into the great Golden Pictures.

It was going to be the third time I'd been on the lot in two days and I was ready for it to be my last. And judging by the time, it was going to be. For good or worse.

A few lights hung off the backs of the buildings, each one over a door. I got myself to the shiniest door there, the new green one that actually stood out like a sore thumb, reached for one of my guns, took it out, and smashed the light bulb over the door with it.

It popped, but not enough to get anyone worked up over.

I pulled out my set of pics and got to work on the door's lock. It was nice, Cardon warning me that the padlock I had shot up hadn't been replaced. It made it so I didn't have to go through the main gate to the place, guns blazing.

I liked the quiet approach much, much better.

I got through the door lock in ten seconds and was inside in twelve.

I pulled out my flash and flicked it on, the beam cutting straight up the long aisle that, not that long ago, I was being chased down. And shot at through.

I had to laugh, thinking about that goon landing straight on his kisser. I could still hear him splat to the concrete.

Then I remembered George. A nice young guy whose only problem was that I had chosen his door to walk into.

I hoped he wasn't dead yet.

After I got the form and called it in to Bella, I would look for George. Unlike Cardon, I figured he had to still be here on the lot. Unless they had already driven him off to Angeles National Forest. Where all the other bodies of LA are dumped.

I made my way through the shelves up to the small office area behind the counter.

Everything was dark, and no one was there. I had the whole place to myself. So I got to work.

Chapter 42

CHARLIE DROVE CAREFULLY ON his way out to Santa Monica.

The last thing he wanted to do was have anything happen to Bella's car or to disappoint Mr. Devin.

Charlie would find Alice for him and bring her back. No matter what it took.

Mr. Devin had given him a job when nobody else would. When he had nothing. And when Charlie was out living on the streets. He wouldn't let Mr. Devin down, no matter what.

Traffic was thick as cars drifted from one lane to another along Wilshire. Charlie kept his eyes on the road and on every car around him, making sure nobody hit him. This run was a lot longer than any run to get bottles for his old man.

But he would find Alice.

No matter what.

And Charlie remembered her well.

Alice Murphy belonged to a family of fighters. Her brothers, and she had five of them, had all pretty much been expelled from school by the time Charlie was ten. And that was saying something.

Alice herself wasn't that much better. Although there was a soft streak inside of her, buried deep. That's what Charlie thought, at least, when he knew her in school. But that soft streak didn't stand much of a chance with brothers like that and a father like she had.

If Charlie's father was a drunk, Alice Murphy's father was a raging drunk. She used to come in to school with bruises on her face and on her arms. She said it was just roughhousing with her brothers, but everyone knew what happened. Her father had a temper.

Her mother died when Alice was in fifth grade, and Charlie remembered the day. The principal had come in to take her out of class, then everyone in the class heard the scream from tiny Alice out in the hall. Charlie still remembered it. It was chilling.

Then she didn't come to school for two weeks after that, and when she did, that's when the bruising started.

So no wonder she had tried to run away from home. At least according to what she said in the letter. And Charlie had every reason to believe it. The Alice he knew was quiet and never said a word. So writing a letter? To a lawyer? That had to have taken something for her. He knew that for a fact.

Chapter 43

I CHECKED OUT ALL the file cabinets by George's counter, but couldn't find any files with Gold or Stan Brown's name on it. I even checked under *S*… for Snake. Yeah, it wasn't there.

Nothing.

Which meant the drawing could be anywhere. Or nowhere.

I doubted that Stan was dumb enough to actually sign a form to get the lighter made up. But that didn't mean that young George didn't make something up himself. He struck me as the conscientious type. At least I hoped.

A record for everything, and everything in its place.

I poked around outside the area of George's counter and found another room off to the side, complete with, once I had switched on the lights, gray walls and about fifty file cabinets.

Fifty.

My heart sank a little lower and I looked up at a clock that hung on the gray wall — 8:53 p.m.

And my heart sank even lower still.

Chapter 44

CHARLIE WAS ONLY A couple of blocks away from the Murphy home.

He knew, because he used to live on the next street over. In the house he grew up in. That his father had kicked him out of.

Charlie didn't feel good about being back in the area, it brought back too many memories. Bad memories. But he did feel good that maybe he was going to help Mr. Devin. And that woman, the mother of the guy who was going to be hanged. There was something to Charlie about saving this guy, even though he didn't know him from Adam. The guy had gotten a raw deal. And Charlie could relate.

Charlie pulled up to the curb in front of a small bungalow with dried weeds for a yard. There was only one light on inside. He got out of Bella's car, the engine snapping and clicking as the hot engine met the cooler air coming in from the ocean.

The house itself was broken-down, its roof wavy under the moonlight and the gray of the porch blending into everything else about the house. The front steps creaked as he hit the first one, and a pack of dogs exploded on the other side of the front door.

Charlie steeled himself and knocked. The dogs went even more insane inside, then a man's gravelly voice yelled over the top of them. "Shut up! Go away!"

Charlie assumed the first was for the dogs, and the second one was directed at him.

Charlie banged on the door again and the howls of the dogs got even louder.

"I said get the hell away!"

Charlie called out. "Mr. Murphy, it's Charlie Moore."

"Charlie who?"

"I'm looking for Alice, Mr. Murphy. Do you know where she is?"

The lock slammed open on the other side, followed quickly by the door itself. And there stood Jack Murphy. He stood even taller than Charlie's six feet, his shoulders the size of a blacksmith's. And Charlie could smell the liquor on him. "What's this about Alice?"

Mr. Murphy stayed on the other side of the screen door, which was good. At least that gave Charlie a little bit of courage. "I'm looking for Alice, Mr. Murphy."

Jack Murphy stared at Charlie. "I know you…"

"Yeah, I'm Ben Moore's son."

Murphy looked at Charlie through his squinted eyes, then he smiled. "Ben said he ran you off." Then Murphy laughed. "Said he ran you off real good. You must really piss him off."

"It doesn't take much."

Murphy laughed again. "You got that right." He wove back and forth a bit, still disoriented. "I've had enough problems with Ben in my life. He has a mean right hook."

Charlie thought back to all the beatings he had taken from his old man, and he didn't have a response for Mr. Murphy. "I need your daughter, Mr. Murphy. I mean I need to find her; where is she?"

"Hell, she left here going on a year ago."

No. "You know where she is?"

"I might. What's in it for me?"

Charlie was surprised Mr. Murphy didn't even care what Charlie wanted her for. He only cared about himself. "I can get you a bottle if you want."

Murphy eyed Charlie suspiciously. "How do you know where to get a bottle? And you're not gonna get me any of that bathtub shit, are you?"

Charlie shook his head. "The guy I'm working for, he'll get you the good stuff."

"I want you to give it to me now. Or are you standing there on my front porch lying to me?"

Mr. Murphy pushed open the screen door a little, looking like he was going to come out. The dogs rushed forward but Murphy kept the door shut just enough. A frazzled, black mutt the size of a sheep, grunting and growling, tried to violently wrestle its way through the door, but thankfully Murphy kept it closed just enough so only its drooling snout snapped out.

Charlie started to get angry. He was not going to let Mr. Murphy push him around. He could tell the man wanted the bottle, and probably no matter how good or bad it was. Charlie had had enough experience to know, liquor was liquor, to anyone who wanted it bad enough.

Charlie looked Mr. Murphy right in his bloodshot and watery eyes. "I don't have it."

"Then get the hell—"

"*But,*" Charlie rolled over him, "I'll bring you two instead. Tomorrow. I promise."

Murphy laughed. "What's a promise?"

Charlie took one step closer to the door, the snapping dog, and the drunken Mr. Murphy, and hoped at his full six foot he looked just a little scary himself. "Something I keep."

Mr. Murphy stood there on the other side of the filthy screen door looking at Charlie, his mouth breathing in air and breathing out heavy alcohol. His lips were dry and cracked. And he looked like a man deciding between hell and salvation. Then he decided, Charlie saw it in his eyes. "You know Cletus?"

Yeah, Charlie knew Cletus. Alice's older brother.

Chapter 45

CARDON SLAMMED HIS HAND on the steering wheel of the car.

"Damn it!"

The small dirt street he was parked on gave no reply but a small breeze that came down from the mountains to his right. To the right where the small white clapboard house of Standish's girlfriend stood, without the Standish kid in it. And no way Cardon could have phoned, because they didn't even *have* one.

"Damn it!"

Cardon started the motor, slammed the car into gear, and swung it around to head back to US66 that would get him back to Pasadena, then back to Los Angeles — about an hour away if he flew.

An hour. And it was already 9:27 p.m.

"Damn it!"

Cardon accelerated to as fast as he dared. With the bad roads he was bound to get a flat, unless he prayed, and he was not exactly the praying kind.

He had gone to the Standish kid's house in Altadena originally and turned up nothing. Nothing except a mother who said if George had left work early, he'd most likely go to his girlfriend's house — in Azusa!

Azusa. Even further away from LA.

Devin had told him not to come. Said it would be a wild-goose chase. But Cardon had been as stubborn as usual. Follow down every lead… as he always had.

"Damn it!"

As Cardon finally turned onto US 66, he thought maybe, just maybe, he'd do things differently next time.

Unfortunately for Miles White, there was no next time.

"Damn it!"

Chapter 46

IN THE SIDE ROOM with the gray walls — and the fifty filing cabinets — after a lot of digging I figured out that everything was filed by the name of the picture.

Which meant that Stan could have given him any name for a fictitious picture. Great.

There were also other files that I couldn't figure out what they had to do with anything. They didn't have picture names, but they had people names. I guessed probably all the directors, costume designers, and people who designed all the sets.

But there was no telling where the drawing could be. Or what regular name or picture name Stan could have given George. Or without a name, where George may have just stuffed it.

Again, if it even existed.

But I had to find it. Otherwise Miles was toast. Unless Charlie found the girl.

Then I realized I was ten minutes past when I should have called Bella. I walked out to the counter area and dialed her.

"Hello?" Bella sounded tight.

"It's me, Devin."

"John! You're late."

"I know, I got busy. Has Charlie called? Or Cardon?"

"No on Charlie," I could tell by her voice she was upset, "And nothing from Cardon either."

I wasn't the only one slacking off on the telephoning in.

"Have you found anything yet?"

I laughed. "A lot of filing cabinets."

"But any drawings?"

"No." I wished I had better news for her. She was taking all of this hard. "There are a lot of files here, and it's going to take me a lot longer to get through the rest of them."

"How long?"

I looked up at the clock to the side of the counter. "Too long."

There was a pause at the other end of the line. "Then what are you going to do?"

"Pray the kid finds the girl. And gets her back to you. When Cardon calls, don't tell him where I'm at. Just that I'm out following leads."

"Why don't you let him help you with the files?"

The logic was sound, if it was anyone other than Cardon. "I think he'd have a problem with how I got in here."

"He knows something is fishy with the case, right?"

"I think so, yeah, but—"

"Police do worse things, John, than trying to figure out who really killed someone."

I wasn't so sure with Cardon. He was pretty straight-up about things. "Well, then still don't tell him I'm here. But gently *suggest* that he gets his butt back here and looks around for George's car. Or George. Or something. Anything. It's all we got, Bella."

"Okay, fine."

I hung up the phone and hoped to God that Charlie found the girl. Because *that* was probably all we really had.

Chapter 47

AS SOON AS BELLA hung up with Devin, she let out a huge sigh.

She sat at her desk, the entire office empty and quiet.

She hoped Devin would find the file. Or that Charlie would call with the girl. Anything.

Then the phone rang. She grabbed it. "Hello?"

It was Cardon. "I'm heading back downtown."

"Did you find the guy at his house?"

"Don't even ask." Voices came from behind Cardon, and loud metal-hitting-metal sounds. "I was in Azusa."

"Azusa? Where is that even?"

"You don't want to know." A loud crash rolled over Cardon's voice. Metal falling onto a concrete floor. "Too far."

"But did you find him?"

"No."

Bella's heart sank. "Then what—"

"I'm heading back to LA right now." Cardon yelled away from the receiver. "*Hey*! I need it now!!"

"What's going on, Cardon?"

"I had a flat."

Bella looked up at the clock. It was 10:35 p.m. "Cardon, you have to get back."

"I know. I was right in front of a service station. I'm in Pasadena and they're working on it right now. Where's Devin?"

Bella wanted to avoid that question. Then she remembered Charlie. "Cardon, we got a letter. From the attorney who represented Miles. It's a letter from a young girl, and she says she was there the night that Liliana was killed. And that she saw a car, and two guys carry her from the car into the restaurant."

"Who?"

"A girl. She said she saw it—"

"No, I mean who gave it to you? The letter."

Bella remembered back to June, and all it took for her to bring the letter to them. Bella hoped she could do something for the young girl. "The secretary to the attorney, Streck, who represented Miles in the case. She said Streck threw away the note and didn't even try to investigate it. Or bring it up at the trial."

"What did the note say?"

"Like I say, that she was there that night."

"Did she say anything about Miles White? That he didn't do it?"

"She said she didn't think either of them looked like Miles."

Cardon exhaled on the other side of the line. "Who's the girl?"

"Her name is Alice Murphy. And Charlie here from the office, he knows her."

"Knows her!?"

Bella smiled as she thought of Charlie. What were the odds? "Yeah."

"What are the odds?"

Bella laughed. "Exactly." She looked up at the clock on the wall and it was 10:37 p.m. Late. She didn't know how all of this would play out, but she hoped at the end of it that Miles' mother was going to have her son back. "He went to find her."

"Well, why didn't you call LAPD?" Cardon was mad.

"Devin didn't think it was a good idea. And honestly, I didn't either. What do you want, us to call Price and Black?"

"You didn't have to call them."

Bella heard Cardon's frustration through the line. "I know…
but word would have gotten back to them, right? And probably
fast."

There was no response from Cardon. Bella hoped he got the
point.

"Where are they at?"

"She's in Santa Monica, and Charlie's gone there to find her."

"That's as far away from me as the moon." He let out another
long sigh. "Okay, I'm coming to you. You have the letter, right?"

Bella closed her eyes. "No. It's with Devin."

"And where exactly is *he*?"

Bella was caught between a rock and a .45 caliber gun. The
gun being Devin's. Well, two of them.

She had to tell Cardon. And hopefully he could help Devin with
the files. If he didn't arrest him first. "He's at Golden Pictures. In
the prop room. Looking for anything he can find on the lighter."

A muffled voice came over the line from the background
somewhere. "We're done."

Dead silence filled the space between Bella and Cardon. "O…
kay… I'll go there before he gets himself in any more trouble. Or
destroys this case before we can even prove anything. The next
time you talk with him, tell him to stop whatever he's doing and
stay put. I'll be there in an hour."

And then the line went dead.

And Bella wished there was something she could do, except
wait.

For more time.

Chapter 48

CHARLIE WAS PANICKED. HE completely forgot to call to Bella.

Now he stood in the phone booth next to Wilshire, hoping he hadn't screwed up too bad.

"Hello!" It was Bella and she sounded — furious.

"It's Charlie..."

"Charlie! Where have you been?!"

"I found her."

"You found her?"

"Yes." He still couldn't believe it himself. But there she was, Alice Murphy, sitting in Bella's Model T pulled right up next to the phone booth. He nodded to Alice, who gave him a tentative nod back.

"What took you so long? You were supposed to call."

"I know, but I had to go to her father's. Then to her brother's, then to another brother, and finally over to—"

"Charlie! I don't care. As long as you have her. You do have her, right?"

"I told you that already." Charlie was frustrated, too. He was scared that he wouldn't find her, and now that he had, he was scared he wouldn't get her there in time. "What time is it?"

"It's eleven fifteen, Charlie. Just get her here. *Now*."

But the Miles guy would be hanged in… forty-five minutes? "Can I talk to Mr. Devin?"

"He's not here, Charlie."

Charlie panicked. "Where is he?"

"He's at the studio. Detective Cardon is heading there right now to get him."

"Are they coming back to the office?"

There was a pause at the other end of the line. "I'm waiting for Devin to call back."

"You don't know when he'll call back??"

"He'll call back. And as soon as he does, I'll have him get back here right away."

"It's not enough time." Charlie thought about where he was. "I'm close to the studio."

"Charlie, don't you dare."

"Why?"

"It's not safe. If Gold is there—"

"How will he even know who I am?"

"Don't you dare."

Charlie did the math in his head and there wouldn't be enough time for Mr. Devin to get to the office once he called in. If he called in. "I'm taking her there, Bella."

"Charlie! Don't you dare!"

"Tell him to meet us at his car."

Mr. Devin's car he could find.

And that was that.

Charlie hung up the phone and ran to Alice in the car. He would get her there.

If it's the last thing he did.

Chapter 49

DEVIN'S BLOOD WENT TO ice.

He looked at the clock on the wall, its little hand on the eleven, its big hand at twenty-seven, and he knew it was too late.

Devin had gone through every file in the outer office and a good number of the ones in the back office. He'd even checked desk drawers, under desks, anywhere George could've filed it.

There was no way he would find the drawing. George had either filed it well, or it never existed to begin with. And it was probably the second.

Devin called Bella.

"Hello??" She sounded frantic.

"It's me. I got nothing."

"Devin — Charlie has the girl."

"He *does*?" That was the first good thing I'd heard in two days.

"He's bringing her there."

"Here? To the studio? How did he think to come here?"

"You were there. And I hadn't heard from you. And Cardon is coming there, too."

Great. A regular ice cream social. And I didn't know if the

lovely Stan was on the lot at all. At least he wouldn't know who the kid was, but... if he'd seen the girl at Liliana's, or if Gold had, or whoever had been there — the girl could be in trouble. "How close is Cardon?"

"He called from Pasadena, an hour ago."

I couldn't believe it. "That's still a ways away. Okay, call the police and tell them there's been a murder at Golden Pictures."

"What?"

"Bella, I don't know if Gold or his security guy is even on the lot, but if they are, and they recognize the girl at all—"

"Devin, we don't even know if they saw her or not."

"She's the only witness. If they did recognize her, and if they see her, they'll kill her. If the cops are here? Maybe it'll make them think twice. Or at least keep them busy for a bit."

"Okay."

"And if Cardon calls in, tell him I'm... heading to Gold's office."

"Wait, Charlie said he'd meet you at your car."

Damn. My car was on the side street and I was not going to wait in the parking lot here for Charlie, hoping he made it in time. There were still a few minutes; I could at least do something. "Tell you what, if Cardon calls, send him to the main parking lot here at the studio and keep an eye out for Charlie and the girl. If he finds them, tell him to call the judge right away. If not, wait there in the parking lot. If Gold and Stan are in Gold's office, I'll meet Cardon back in the parking lot. If they're not, Gold has a safe in his office and I'm going to take a peek inside to see if there's anything about Liliana in it... just in case."

"In case what?"

"In case the kid doesn't make it here with the girl. I don't trust anything, and we need everything we can get." I looked up at the clock: 11:29 p.m. Who knows, between the girl and anything in the safe, maybe Judge James would have something he could stop the noose with.

At least that's what I was hoping.

As I hung up the phone — and ran.

Chapter 50

The entire building was dead inside. And dark.

I got to the interior reception area just outside Gold's office and there was no beautiful blonde around and no light coming from under the door to his office. I pulled one of my guns anyway.

You never knew.

I grabbed the golden knob on the golden door, gave it a twist, and slowly pushed it open.

It was quiet inside, but light came in from the set of windows behind his desk, which faced out onto the lot.

I looked around the rest of the office and apparently it was red day today. Every red flower imaginable stood on all the tables, the credenza, and against the bar. Most of them were roses. Which I hate. Not the looks of them, the smell.

They smelled like a funeral.

I closed the door behind me, my gun still up and ready. Although I wasn't sure why, with nobody in there and all.

I guess just habit.

The safe was still to the left of Gold's unoccupied desk, and I headed for it.

Chapter 51

CARDON PULLED UP TO the main gate of Golden Pictures and flashed his badge to the young guard.

The guard, a young kid about twenty and with pimples, came out with a clipboard and looked at Cardon's badge, then up at him with a smile. "What can I do for you, officer?"

"Detective." Cardon wasn't in the mood.

The guard shied a bit. "Detective, I'm sorry."

"I was in earlier, about a disappearance. I just need to—"

"Do you have an appointment?" The kid looked down at his clipboard, then back up at Cardon.

"No. I don't have an appointment." Cardon needed to get in there before Devin did any more damage, and rescue him from himself.

The kid went back to the booth. "Let me just call someone…"

To Cardon, it didn't look like there was anyone left on the lot. It was deserted.

The kid got on the phone and tried one number. Nothing. Then another.

Cardon was getting impatient. "Look, I know where I'm going."

"Just one more, sir." And the kid hung up his phone and tried another.

Chapter 52

THE PHONE ON GOLD'S desk rang, jerking Devin away from Gold's safe.

He immediately got up and stood in front of the massive desk, staring at the phone.

He had gotten the first number in the combination for the safe, a five, before the phone rang and he jerked the dial, ruining his current run at it. Now he'd have to start again. But he waited there in front of the desk until the phone would stop.

It finally did.

Just as something caught his eye outside the massive window in back of the desk.

Three men, two of them huge, one of them medium-sized, dragged what looked like either a movie dummy or a real person, by the shoulders across 7th Street that ran straight up to the back of the lot.

The group got to the corner of a sound stage marked *28*, then under a single lightbulb illuminating a small doorway to the inside, then they dragged the person, and themselves, inside.

The three guys standing looked remarkably like Stan, and

Gold's two goons. The one being dragged was painfully thin… and looked about the size of a certain junior prop master.

Devin got to the office door in a second and had his gun out a split second after that. Heading to the sound stage below.

Chapter 53

THE GUARD STOOD THERE in his little stucco-colored booth, staring at the phone. "The director of security isn't answering his phone either. Or Mr. Gold. They're on the lot somewhere." The guard turned to Cardon. "You said you had an appointment?"

Cardon didn't like the sound of that. That Gold and his security guy were on the lot.

It meant they may see Devin.

Cardon looked at the kid, put his car in gear, then smiled. "Don't worry, I know where I'm going." And he hit the gas. Hard.

Cardon thought he heard the kid yelling after him.

Over the sound of his car motor.

Accelerating.

Chapter 54

I RAN UP THE smooth asphalt of 7th Street, the single, exterior lights of each sound stage lighting the dark path in front of me until I got to *28*.

When I got to the sound stage, nobody was around up and down 7th, or down a narrow cross street that headed back into the middle of the lot.

I took two more breaths to quiet my breathing and tried the door. Locked.

Damn it.

I put the gun back in its holster and reached into my inside jacket pocket next to it. A small, folded packet of felt that held my picks waited inside.

I pulled out a tension wrench and pick, then got down on one knee.

That's when light exploded in my eyes, just as something very hard hit me in the head.

It's the last thing I remembered.

Except the sound of a very large bell ringing.

Chapter 55

CARDON GOT TO THE main parking lot and there was no Charlie yet.

Instead of standing there in the open, waiting for the young guard to come along and be a nuisance, Cardon decided to walk to the edge of a small street ahead, to blend into the shadows and wait for Charlie to show.

Except when he got to the small side street, he heard a noise from down at the other end of the street.

Under a single light above a door leading into a large building, Cardon saw a big man dragging another man in through the door by the shoulders.

The light was faint, and the shadow from the guy above blocked out most of the guy on the ground, but if Cardon used just enough imagination, the guy being dragged was about the size of Devin. "Damn it."

Cardon took one look back at the parking lot and there was still no Charlie.

"Damn it."

Then Cardon shook his head, drew his gun, and kept to the

shadows as he ran down the side street toward the door at the far end under the single light.

Chapter 56

CHARLIE PULLED THE MODEL T up to the gate as a young guard stood inside his booth dialing a phone.

The guard motioned to Charlie to wait right there as he was waiting on the line, hung it up, and then tried another number. The guy looked frantic, and definitely occupied.

Charlie looked at Alice next to him, then out and into the lot. Mr. Devin was nowhere to be seen. He wondered if Bella had told him that they were coming. Or maybe he never talked to her, and maybe they'd have to find him.

Charlie looked up into the small booth and, just over the guard's shoulder, was a clock. It said 11:42 p.m. "No…." Then he waved to the guard. "Hey, did a Detective Cardon come in here?"

The guard looked at Charlie, shocked. "Yeah. How did you know?"

"I'm supposed to meet him."

The young guard now looked ticked off. "What is this, a convention?"

He dialed another number on his phone and turned his back on Charlie. Just over the guard's back, the clock now read 11:43 p.m.

"Forget it." He looked at Alice. "Do you trust me?"

She looked at Charlie. "I hardly know you."

Charlie shrugged his shoulders. "Well, you better now." Charlie dropped the car in gear and drove straight onto the lot, and thought he heard the guard yelling after him. Over the sound of Bella's Model T accelerating.

Chapter 57

CARDON WALKED UP TO the door with the light above it. The one that Devin had just been dragged through.

Cardon decided right then and there he really was going to kill Devin.

After he hopefully saved him.

"You jackass."

Cardon tried the door and the knob turned. Then he quietly opened the door a crack. Seeing nobody on the other side, he opened it just enough and squeezed himself through.

And shut the door behind him.

Chapter 58

CHARLIE QUICKLY PULLED INTO the main parking lot, and there was nobody around.

Through the windshield he could see directly up a small, narrow street, to a light on the side of a building in the distance, just above a door.

Detective Cardon went into the door.

"Come on!" Charlie jumped out of the car on his side, then ran to the other side and practically pulled Alice out, dragging her up the narrow street.

"Charlie, slow down!"

Charlie didn't break stride but held her hand tighter as they kept running toward the door, getting closer to it by the second. Her hand was warm. And as he held it tighter so she had to follow, he realized that he'd never actually held a girl's hand before.

It was an odd place to do it, he thought, in the dark, running, on the Golden Pictures lot.

He almost smiled as he ran even faster, trying to get to Cardon before the time ran out.

Chapter 59

COLD HIT ME IN the face like ice.

Then I felt water dropping to my chest and realized — I was alive. Well wasn't that just grand.

Through the haze that was my consciousness at the moment, I looked around, and from what I could tell, I was inside the sound stage I had just tried to pick my way into.

My hands were tied, rather tightly and securely in back of me, as I sat on some kind of chair. The chair had a high back that supported me, with the small straight legs of the thing running down to a red and gold oriental rug beneath me. I was in a dining room. Or rather, a movie set where half of it was a dining room and the other half was missing, completely opening out into a large and darkened space beyond. The rest of the open sound stage.

Gold and Stan sat in director's chairs a little out in front of me, out in the sound stage, while Gold's two huge goons stood directly in back of them. Beyond the four of them was the large opening of the rest of the sound stage, with a bunch of individual, fake movie walls scattered near the far end of the place. There were pieces of bathroom walls, bits of a bedroom, and even what looked like walls from a grand ballroom from another century.

Overall, it looked like a storage area for unused sets.

Then I looked to my left and there was George, the assistant prop master, lying on the rug next to me, tied up, with a gag in his mouth. And thankfully his eyes were open. Full of terror, but he was okay.

Then to my right, down on the rug but sitting up, was Max. Also tied up, and also gagged. But he didn't look terrified. As he looked up at me, he looked just plain ticked. No. Make that enraged.

I understood.

I couldn't believe I had let one of the goons get the drop on me.

"Mr. Devin, so good of you to show up." Gold smiled from his director's chair. It was the first time I'd seen the man smile. "It makes things much easier."

My head hurt bad. "Look, Gold, I can see we've gotten off on the wrong foot here." I decided to try out my charm. "Why don't you untie me and let me go for old time's sake."

Gold smiled. "I've only known you a little over a day. That hardly counts for old times."

"Well, maybe I have a different sense of time than you."

One thing I didn't catch at first. My two guns lay on the dining room table next to me.

This kept getting worse.

Then I saw Cardon. Stepping between the fake walls on the far end of the sound stage.

***

Cardon flashed between two of the floating movie walls at the far end of the sound stage from where Devin was tied up.

Decorated on their front sides to be walls for different parts of a house, on the backsides they were just plain two-by-fours, with small supports on both sides, with wheels at the bottom so they could be pushed into place.

Luckily, they provided great cover for Cardon as he tried to get closer to the group of men.

From what Cardon could see as he ran through the open spaces between the walls, there were four men in a cluster between Devin and him, two of them looking pretty large, and two of them seated on director's chairs.

Then he noticed one guy sitting on the floor to the side, and another lying near Devin. Both of them looked like they were tied up. Maybe one of them was the missing prop guy. Somehow Cardon had a feeling it was. But he wasn't sure who the other one was.

Cardon looked at his watch. It was 11:47 p.m.

***

I got a sudden burst of good feelings with Cardon hanging around at the edges. The cavalry. Except I wasn't sure how much he knew. I figured I better let him know, so he could just shoot somebody and end this little party. I kicked up my voice a couple of levels. "Hey Gold, did you know there was a little girl there when you met Liliana at her restaurant?"

Gold looked at Stan, then at me, then back at Stan again.

Stan kept cool, but I could see a quick flash in his black little eyes. If they were in the car when Liliana and the girl got to the restaurant that night, they probably saw the girl. But they didn't know everything. "Yeah, funny thing, Liliana gave her a ride as far as the restaurant. When they got there, your car was there. The girl left, which I'm sure you saw, but then she came back. Apparently she didn't like the look of your car. She had a bad feeling about it. Pretty good for a kid, huh?"

Then Gold leaned in to Stan to whisper something.

"Speak up, boys… you're going to kill me, right? What does it matter what I know or not?"

Gold looked at me. The hate in his eyes was hard. Then he smiled. And laughed. "Why not, Devin. I always say if you're going to screw someone, let them know exactly how you're going to do it."

"Well — we got her, Gold, and she's talking to the LAPD right now."

Then Gold's smile went hard like his eyes. "Then why are you here, Devin? You're bluffing. If you had her, you wouldn't be here with me right now. And you sure as hell wouldn't have been creeping around."

"She came back, Gold. She saw you."

And I hoped Cardon was listening.

***

The space was large and dark, Cardon thought, as he looked around the wall he hid behind. At least it was dark at his end and he hoped he could get closer without any of them seeing him. But unfortunately there was a lot of open space between Cardon and the group of men. Not exactly close for shooting, and too far to run across without getting shot yourself.

"She saw you carry Liliana into the restaurant." Devin spoke loud, like he was trying to wake the dead, his voice getting swallowed up in the vast, open area above them. But it was enough for Cardon to hear. "And it was by the shoulders and ankles. Level with me, Gold, was Liliana dead by then?"

Cardon heard a small sound from the door to the outside.

He turned and saw Charlie, the kid from Devin's office, walk in through the door to the outside — followed by a girl.

No.

Cardon watched as Charlie recognized him and opened his mouth to speak.

Cardon snapped his finger to his lips while waving them off with his other hand that held his gun. Charlie and the girl immediately stopped and kept themselves still. Good. At least there was that.

"You can tell me, Gold. I'm not going anywhere."

Charlie heard Devin's voice and looked around for him. Cardon wanted to strangle the kid. He couldn't believe he'd brought the girl here. Bella must have told the kid where they were. The exact place *not* to bring the girl.

Luckily the kid and girl were both covered by some of the other floating walls. For now, at least. If they didn't move.

Or talk. Or make any kind of sound.

Cardon looked at them both as they looked at him. Charlie pointed at the girl, vigorously.

Cardon nodded to him.

"What's the matter, cat got your tongue?" Devin practically shouted from the other end of the sound stage.

Cardon motioned for the kids to get the hell back out the door.

Charlie motioned to his wrist, as if there were a strap watch fastened around it and Cardon again pointed — vigorously — *get the hell out of here.*

"You killed her, didn't you Gold…"

Charlie peaked around the wall and his eyes went wide.

Cardon was going to strangle the kid.

"Actually, I did. I didn't even have Stan do it. That bitch was going to cost me."

Cardon's heart sank. Not because he just heard Gold confess to killing Liliana McGann, but because he saw in Charlie's eyes something shift. And he knew the kid was not going to leave until he got Devin out of there. A kid.

That's what Cardon's life had become at that moment. So he had better save Devin.

Before the kid tried and got all of them dead.

***

"So what did poor Max do to you?" I looked over at Max and he still sat there to the side, looking more and more angry by the minute. I think he also knew that we were all dead unless something happened.

And that's why I was hoping Cardon would make something

happen, and quick.

Gold got his great bulk up from his director's chair and looked down at Max like a menacing, evil force. "Max actually did nothing to me. Except exactly what I wanted." Then Gold laughed and looked back at me. "It's funny, Devin, you work around pictures long enough, and you can tell what's going to happen even before they start. You know what I did back east?"

Great, he was a talker. "I heard rumors."

"Well, let me tell you, the other thing I've learned is that rumors are mostly true. At least the bad ones. But I digress. See, I had a problem with Liliana; she just didn't understand movie making."

"You mean she didn't understand when to keep her mouth shut and let you keep taking her money."

Gold looked at me. "What *her money*? It was all mine. I put up all the risk — I get all the reward."

I saw Cardon make his way behind another wall, closer. "You didn't give her what she was worth." I said it loud, to cover him.

Gold looked at me funny. Then let it pass. "I have a lot of people to pay for here, Devin. It's like this: Liliana's pictures help to keep a lot of people employed."

"I heard your studio was on the ropes. Lose a little bit of money, did you?"

Gold's eyes went to ice and his eyes flicked to the lowly minions standing around him. He looked like a proud man who didn't particularly like getting his kingship questioned. He reached out his hand to Stan, and Stan took a gun out from his belt. Gold took it, and I could see it made him feel powerful. "My studio has no problems whatsoever." He thumped his chest with the gun. "I built it into what it is today." Thumped it like an ape.

"That's good, Gold. You got a good studio here. And everybody better stay in line."

He walked toward me, "You know the problem with people like you?" until he stood right in front of me.

"I'm guessing you're going to—"

Gold smashed me in the face with the gun.

My head snapped to the side, the gun heavier than it looked. Then I saw white for a second until that started to resolve itself into floating little bits of white. And I couldn't hear too good either.

Yep, I had him right where I wanted him.

Then Gold hauled off and smashed me on the other side of the face. This time black started forming at the edges of my vision and tried to rush into the center, choking off whatever awareness I had left from the first hit.

I shook my head, trying to clear anything I could.

Then I saw a wall, to the left of where I saw Cardon was — move. What the...?

"So you want to know what I did? I hadn't planned on killing you; I offered you to go free, but no... you had to come back. And all I was going to do was have Max kill the kid over there, who made him the lighter, and then have Stan kill Max. Everything tight, nothing loose."

I was at least conscious enough to open my mouth again. "Max didn't have the kid make the lighter for you, Stan did."

Gold slugged me again and, amazingly, I didn't lose it. But Gold looked like he was. Good. I was getting to him. That's always my plan — wear 'em down.

I just wished Cardon would get a move on. Before I actually was dead.

"That's why I had Max come to you in the first place, to talk you out of trying to clear that little nobody Liliana shacked up with." He looked over at Max, still sitting on the floor. "The *M* on the lighter was for Manzione, that was my thought at first. I hate that bastard. But the more I thought about it, Manzione would come up with an alibi..." Gold laughed. "Because he didn't do it. So I set Max up by giving him an errand that night near the restaurant. So he was there in the area."

Max's eyes went wider and angrier.

"But then those idiot cops grabbed up the little nobody."

"His name is Miles." I offered.

"Whatever. So the minute I heard you were snooping around,

I had Max here make you an offer: back off on the investigation, for a lot of work. Like he was trying to cover up his own crime." Gold looked down at Max. "Sorry, Max, it's just business." Then Gold looked back at me.

I looked down at Max myself. He hadn't done a thing all along.

Then I could see that, somehow, Max had worked his legs beneath himself as he sat.

"Look at me!" Gold yelled.

I looked back up, into Gold's black eyes. There was only hate in there.

"I gave you a chance. There was something I liked about you. Maybe I could see you could play dirty, too, and I liked that. But you threw it back in my face. So… I'm going to kill you myself. With Stan's gun." He nodded toward my .45s on the table next to me. "Then we're going to use your guns to shoot both Max and the kid. And Stan? He's a hero. And me? Ever thankful as always."

I really raised my voice, loud. "Fine — then go ahead and kill me!"

Something shifted in Gold's eyes. He looked deeply into mine, then he looked in back of himself. Then he looked back at me. "Why are you talking loud?"

I smiled. "I do that when I'm scared."

He didn't believe me, and his eyes never left mine. "You've been doing that since you opened your mouth." Gold looked left, and then right. Then he looked to the two goons and nodded in back of them.

They drew their guns and headed back into the darkness… right toward the scattered fake walls.

***

Cardon heard the silence at the other end of the sound stage and didn't like it.

"Where are you going, boys?" Devin's voice. "You going off to check on things?"

Then a slap sounded from where Devin was, except it sounded more like metal to flesh.

Cardon looked over at Charlie, and while Cardon at least had a gun, the kid had nothing. Except a young girl next to him.

Then the kid did something crazy — he moved his wheeled wall to the right, pushed the girl behind the other wall, then took his own wall and broke further away from Cardon.

Damn it.

Cardon looked quickly out and around from his own wall. The two goons were running at the kid's wall, their guns out.

Then one goon shot, and then the other, directly into the wall, and they kept on firing. The kid dropped to his knees and kept pushing.

The kid had distracted them enough, so Cardon leaned out further and shot the guy nearest him, then the other turned to Cardon just in time to see Cardon's gun fire.

Cardon's shot hit him square in the chest and knocked him to the ground.

Then a shot rang out and Cardon heard a zip past his left ear and felt the heat of the round.

Then another shot and another.

Cardon saw one of the guys from the director's chairs firing at him.

Cardon dropped to one knee and returned fire.

***

Charlie was kind of stupid. At least that's what he told himself as he kept pushing his wall closer to where he heard the gunfire coming from.

He wasn't going to let Mr. Devin die. No way he was going to let that happen.

He felt like he had superhuman strength as he kept low and kept pushing at the base of the wall, and as far as he could against the left corner. That's where he ended up after the first shots

238

punched through the wall; then strength took over as he pushed and pushed toward where the shots were still coming from.

It was the only way to draw their fire so Detective Cardon could shoot.

At least that's the way he saw it in the westerns. Charlie loved Buck Jones.

And then Charlie couldn't believe he was even thinking about that.

No more shots hit his wall, which was great. But that meant they were going somewhere else. Either at Detective Cardon or Mr. Devin, so Charlie pushed even harder toward where the last of the gunshots came from.

Until his wall ran into something that stopped him.

Then Charlie looked just beyond the edge of the wall next to him and saw a hand on the floor.

A hand with a gun still in it.

Charlie didn't even think about it.

He reached for the gun.

Chapter 60

I SAW THE LAST two shots fired simultaneously by Stan and Cardon, and they had both gone down. Hard.

They'd gotten each other.

Stan lay on the concrete floor, a third of his head now missing.

And Cardon? He was a ways away but he hadn't moved since he got hit. I don't know where he took the shot but he lay still, face down, right next to the wall he had been firing from.

And he hadn't moved an inch.

Gold had me on my feet, standing behind me.

My hands were still tied in back of me, and my ankles tied below so there wasn't a lot I could do about Gold's arm above me, Stan's gun right next to my ear.

Gold hadn't fired a shot yet, I think just waiting to see who was still standing. So far it was just me and him. And whoever was behind the ghost wall that kept coming toward us. I wondered if the guard out front had somehow come in. I doubted it. He would have said something. Not walked a wall toward a bunch of gunshots.

George still lay to my left on the floor, while Max still sat on the floor to my right.

All the gun smoke drifted up in the large, open space, and gave it even more of a ghostly appearance. Or it could have just been Stan and the two goon's ghosts flying off to… well, not Heaven.

I just hoped Cardon's ghost wasn't in there along with them. He still hadn't moved and I was getting worried. Hell, I was a lot worried. The only one who had a gun was Gold. And we already knew he was ready to do any killing he needed to.

"You, behind the wall, come out."

"Don't!" I yelled out.

That got me a smack to the head again with Stan's damn gun.

I was going to have to shove that thing in Gold's mouth before I was done with this. And then kick him in the damn teeth.

Gold put on his best nice voice. "Come on out. We're done."

A foot stepped out and away from the wall, followed by a leg, and then a body. Charlie.

Shit.

Shit shit shit. "Charlie — get out of here!"

Gold smashed the gun into my head again and I dropped to the floor. I smashed my shoulder, then rolled over to see Gold leveling the gun at Charlie. "Okay, kid, come on over here."

Then Charlie pulled his hand out from behind his back and leveled a gun at Gold.

I couldn't believe it. "Charlie, *no!*"

"Listen to the man, Charlie! You don't want to do that. You don't want to do that, son. Now… just… put down the gun."

"Charlie, please, just…" I had to talk him out of this, get him out of there safe, "Set the gun down and run."

"He's not going to do that, Devin. Are you now, Charlie?"

My mind raced. "Charlie… just… please, listen to me. You do not want to be a part of this."

"Mr. Devin," Charlie's voice was cracking, "Are you all right?"

I could see the gun he held shaking. He'd never stand a chance against Gold. Maybe he could, maybe Gold couldn't even hit a barn, but I didn't want Charlie there — at all. "I'm all right, Charlie.

We're just working things out."

"Just come here, son."

"Don't you dare, Charlie."

Gold aimed the gun at me.

"*Hey!*" Charlie yelled out, then he fired once into the air.

Charlie then brought the gun slowly down to aim it at Gold.

I wasn't close enough to Gold. I started to inch myself toward him, to hook him with my feet somehow, just as Gold pulled back the hammer on his gun.

I yelled, "*No!*"

Then Max shot up off the floor and launched himself toward the gun, just as the gun itself went off.

Max spun in the air and hit the floor as I shot myself the last bit to hook Gold by the feet, bringing him down to the floor hard. His head slammed on the concrete and bounced, just as I got my size twelves as close as I could to him, then drove the fronts of them right into his temple.

Then he didn't move.

Even after I switched to his mouth and felt and heard his teeth break, even after I kept kicking until blood ran down all sides of his head, and even as I felt a hand on the side of my head and I looked up.

"*Charlie!!*"

Charlie leaned down over me. "Are you okay, Mr. Devin?"

"Am *I* okay? Let me look at you — are you okay, boy?"

I couldn't believe it.

I couldn't believe it. I couldn't believe it.

Quick, check him for blood.

I'd seen enough wounds in the war where somebody didn't even realize they were hit — five times — until they just dropped. "Let me see you."

I was still tied and could have ripped the things off me.

"Stand back."

"What?"

"*I said stand back!!*"

Charlie scooted away from me, dazed, looking at me like I was a crazy man.

"Now turn around. Turn around!"

Charlie slowly turned around, looking as scared as he should be. But there was no blood. There was no blood.

Oh God, there was no blood.

I let my head back to the cold concrete and I breathed.

I think I breathed.

I must have breathed. Because the black that had started to form in my eyes started to fade away... to just what lay in front of me. Then I remembered — "God. Charlie get these off me!"

And Charlie was already untying my hands and then my feet.

Then I got up and ran, as fast as I could, past Max and Stan, past the goons, past Cardon lying on the concrete floor, and I ran out the door until I ran straight to the only place I could think of, flying upstairs and flying through black doors and golden doors until I finally stood behind the great desk of the king himself and made a call.

As it turned out.

Just—

In—

Time.

Chapter 61

IT WAS HOT STANDING outside the Meck.

I looked ahead at Mrs. White, waiting at the small door cut into the chain-link fence that surrounded the prison, her gaze focused on the small metal door cut into the great concrete wall fifty yards inside.

The door her son would come out at any minute.

Two guards waited on the other side of the chain-link fence from her, the barbed wire stretched out above them, trailing up and down the full length of the fence, sparkling in the sun.

I was happy for the woman. I was happy about a lot.

Charlie stood to my right, and June, the girl from Streck's office, stood to my left, Bella just beyond her. They deserved to be here. To see this.

Mrs. White looked back at all of us and waved. I nodded back to her.

The others waved.

Bella and I had driven everybody up.

It had been two days since the dustup at Golden Pictures. I guess it took the prison people that long to unwind things when they pretty much had a noose around Miles' neck.

I'd had to make the call myself.

Lucky enough, the Judge believed me after Gold had essentially confessed in front of us.

The past two days had been quiet ones for all of us.

And Miles was free. Or at least he would be once he walked out that chain-link door.

Gold had lived, unfortunately. Although he was going to need dentures from now on.

That felt good at least. I could still feel his teeth give way in front of my feet.

I guess maybe I could call myself a dentist now.

I looked to my right, past Charlie, and Max stood there. He'd only got hit in the shoulder, thank God, on his way to knocking the gun away from being pointed at Charlie. He saved the kid's life. I'd be thankful to him forever for that.

I still couldn't forgive Charlie.

Trying to get himself killed.

But I had a new respect for the kid. It's why he stood right next to me. I wouldn't let him out of my sight now.

The metal door in the concrete wall that surrounded the Meck opened, and out walked Miles. His mother waved softly from this side of the chain-link fence.

Fifty yards. Not so long a distance in the end, I guessed.

Miles walked steadily across the yard, a small brown bag in his hand.

His suit was black, with a small white stripe running up and down it. It looked pretty nice. Maybe it was his last memory of Liliana.

A last nice suit, bought on her dime.

That made me think of Liliana.

Seemed of everyone wanting her for her money, maybe Miles had the least eye on it. I did believe him that he loved her.

And Liliana deserved that, at least. From someone.

As Miles walked toward the chain-link fence, he looked up into the sky and closed his eyes. The sun must've felt good on him.

On his face.

To be honest, it felt good on me, too. I felt warm.

And that had nothing to do with the family I saw now to my left and right. Bella, June, Charlie, and now Max.

It was a ragtag bunch, but I guess it was my bunch now.

"Does it feel good?"

I looked in back of me, at Cardon.

He had a huge white bandage on the right side of his head, and the way he talked about it, the damn thing still hurt like someone hit him in the head with a hammer.

Luckily it was only a bullet.

And also lucky that the bullet only grazed him. From what the doctor said, if it had been a hair to the left, he would've had the same third of his head missing like Stan did.

I looked at Cardon. "Come here."

I shifted to my right and made a space between me and June. Then Cardon came up to stand with us.

Miles finally made it to the chain-link fence. One of the guards there unlocked the door and swung it open, and Miles went through. Into his mother's arms.

Both of them held each other for a good long time. Their shoulders moved up and down a lot. I guess they were crying.

I looked over at Bella and June, and tears were coming down on both of them. I looked to my right and Charlie's cheek was dry. Mostly. Except the damp streak that still remained where he had wiped away his own tears.

Me? There were no tears.

Miles' mother took her son away from the fence and away from the Meck. They walked past all of us, toward her old truck parked in the lot behind us.

As they walked past, Mrs. White looked at me, tears in her eyes, and mouthed the words *Thank you.*

I tipped my head to her, and was happy we could help.

We all stood there for another minute. All of us. Nobody

saying a thing.

Then we turned around together and headed to the cars.

It was a good day.

And the sun shone down hot, and bright, on all of us.

Enjoy Devin?

Then grab another — check out the other books and stories in the series:

John Devin, PI — The Novels
    Red is for Blood (Book 1)
    Black is for Hate (Book 2)
    Gold is for Greed (Book 3)

John Devin, PI — Short Stories
    Sunshine (No. 1)
    Bennie (No. 2)

Could you help out?

A writer's success is based a lot on word of mouth. If you enjoyed this book, please consider leaving an honest review at your favorite retailer, Goodreads, or any other place that great readers gather.

Even a line or two can make all the difference in the world for me, and helps with every writer's greatest wish — to gather a loyal bunch of readers, just like you.

With great appreciation — Michael

YOUR FREE BOOK IS WAITING

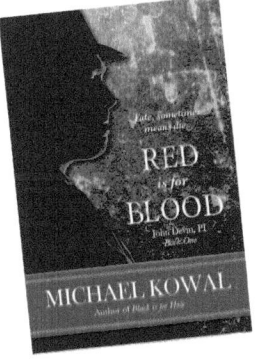

It's 1930s Los Angeles and ex-Marine, and current PI, John Devin tackles his first case... to get back a very big diamond, for a pain in the neck friend.

But the diamond leads Devin on a chase through LA that eventually leads to Chinatown - and the leader of its underworld.

Sometimes people are brought together for a reason - and sometimes the reason... is to die.

★ ★ ★ ★ ★

"Grabs you from the beginning and doesn't let up."

INCLUDES - The Bonus Story: Bennie!
A batch of stolen money leads Devin straight to Bennie... one of my favorite characters in Red is for Blood.

Your free novel - Red is for Blood - is waiting for you,

along with the short story Benny, at:

kowalkowal.com/free-book

Get Them Now!

And keep reading for a sample of

Red is for Blood...

About The Author

Michael Kowal's short fiction appears in multiple volumes of the award winning Fiction River original anthology series, and his John Devin, PI mystery series is available in stores everywhere. He lives on the central Oregon coast with his wife.

Check in with him online at kowalkowal.com and sign up there to be a part of his VIP List for — news, new releases, giveaways, special offers — and even the occasional free story.

Red is for Blood - Sample

Keep reading for the opening Chapters of Book 1 in the John Devin, PI series:

Red is for Blood

And for more about John Devin — and of course all of Michael Kowal's books — visit:

kowalkowal.com

Chapter 1

The fist came at me a split second to midnight, broke my nose at the stroke of, then I heard the band below break into "Jingle Bells." It all smashed together — the fist, my nose, the band, and the pool I was now plummeting toward.

Yeah, the one two stories below me.

It was December 21, 1929.

Merry Christmas to me.

Time slowed like a clock held in mud and that pretty much described my brain at the moment. Fuzzed, slowed, and not thinking too properly. Except I did think of one thing: I hope it's the deep end of the pool.

I hit hard on my back and the water slammed me like concrete. Air shot out of me like a cannon spitting flame, then the cold water rushed in over me.

Numbed, I slowly dropped three, five, and then finally ten feet into the water, until my back softly hit the solid flat surface of the bottom.

Yeah, I'd made it. The deep end.

It was cold, muffled, and wet down here. Not entirely bad because here nobody was trying to kill me. I opened my eyes, and through the hazy and darkened ten feet of water, saw the edges of the pool above. They were rimmed with Christmas lights and the dark bodies of people who stood in front of them, everyone probably wondering who had decided to take a swim.

Not that they were concerned or anything.

I lay there, on the bottom of the pool, relishing the quiet. It's amazing how still everything is in the water, surrounded by something that doesn't care whether you live or die.

Then a thin, dark, wisping snake of red rose in the water above me. My own blood courtesy of my smashed nose. A thin little reminder from my body that it wanted what was up there.

The air that would keep it alive.

Although my brain wasn't sure it wanted to join in that decision.

It was a fight between the two, my brain and my body, the body being the sensible one that wanted to follow the blood topside. My brain, on the other hand, was having its doubts.

It wanted to stay. It was calm down here and what waited above for me was not something it wanted to face. I had gotten into something that I shouldn't, had always sworn I wouldn't, but just this time, just this time only... I did it for the money.

I had to.

Maybe I didn't want to go back up. What it came down to was I had picked a hell of a way to make a living and my brain was lodging a complaint at the moment. Smart one, that brain.

But if I'd listened to it all these years, I would have been dead a hundred times — times twenty. So I went with my gut, as I always did, and pushed my hurt and slammed body off the bottom.

I knew where to go, just follow the trail of my blood back to civilization.

Or what passed for it.

It was late December 1929 and there didn't seem to be a hell of a lot of civilization left these days.

The whole world had started to crack into hell after the crash two months ago. But there was still hope heading into the start of 1930. The hope of the damned, I figured. All of them up there, that's what they celebrated. Me, down here? It seemed the perfect place to close out the '20s. Up there? They all knew what was coming. They just didn't want to admit it. Yet.

But I knew.

So maybe that's why my brain didn't want to head up, but I did anyway.

Back into the city of pain and bright lights.

My home.

Los Angeles.

Chapter 2

I broke the surface to "Jingle Bells," the crowd singing, and a hand ripping me out of the pool by my hair.

Apparently the whole by-the-hair thing didn't matter to anyone, because they just kept drinking, grabbing and grinding each other, everyone well-lubed with the illegal booze that didn't exist.

Welcome to the end of 1929.

The person pulling me up by my hair was Half-a-house. At least that's what I called him. Big as half a house and ugly as a tenement, he had a mustache that tried to make him look like Clark Gable.

It didn't work.

He was the personal bodyguard of one Skyler Gold, the guy I had just been peeking at. Half-a-house grinned at me with a rack of teeth that said I was dead, or at least that I'd soon want to be. "What are you doing here?"

My feet didn't seem to be touching the ground and I was six-feet-and-a-hair as my mother always said. My hair didn't feel too good. "Drip-drying, you mind?"

He slugged me in the gut with his free hand just to get my attention. "I said, what are you doing here. Up there?"

He motioned back to the balcony that he had just thrown me off of. Black wrought iron surrounded it, all curves and thin shapes. It led to two open, white-painted French doors that further led into one of the penthouse suites of the new Hollywood Royal Hotel.

The hotel where apparently all of Los Angeles' best and brightest celebrated Christmas this year.

The central pool was lit and crowded with reds and greens, sparkles, black tuxedoes, jazz, champagne, and highballs. Everything loose and easy, lubed and cocked, flapping away the night like crazed fools running straight into a burning building. Christmas for adults.

I just wanted the hell out of there right now. "I was looking for my wife."

"You don't got no ring."

Half-a-house was observant. "I threw it at her when I kicked her out."

"Then why you lookin' for her?"

I hate logic. Especially from idiots.

"Why don't you let me down and we can talk, civilized, if you know what that is."

Apparently he didn't because instead of letting me drop nice and easy he rammed my head toward the deck and the rest of me followed.

My face plowed straight into the stylish Mexican fiesta-colored tile that surrounded the pool, its second smashing of the night.

I hate this business.

Through the pain and with the energetic energy of the no-fun, twenty-eight-year-old, six-feet, hundred-and-eighty-five-pound ex-Marine that I was — I pile drived my fist straight up into his crotch.

And it slammed into something as hard as a battleship bulkhead.

My knuckles blew out with pain and I just couldn't believe it. He couldn't be that much of a man.

Half-a-house smiled down at me, his bright white teeth just visible under the brim of his light tan fedora.

Then he grabbed my head again, pulled it up knee-high, and as the music dashed into an uphill rag, as the dames and penguins danced off into oblivion, and as I wished like hell I was in some other line of work, Half-a-house's tan-trousered knee ran straight at my face for the final knockout.

And as the knee came up to hit me, a man stepped out from beside Half-a-house and looked straight at me. He wore a white straw hat, a perfect blue suit, and something that didn't really fit into this crowd of swells the color of snow, he was Asian. Not just Asian. Chinese.

I knew Chinese.

And I didn't recognize him.

Then white exploded in my mind and everything went dark.

My brain, it seemed, had finally gotten what it wanted.

Peace.

And quiet.

The quiet of the dead.

Chapter 3

I woke wet, cold, and tied at the neck to the red spokes of a smart-looking tan Packard parked along Wilshire. Tied with my own tie. The joke wasn't lost on me.

Cold concrete lay beneath me trying to suck out what little heat I had left in my body. If you listened to the promotions people, Los Angeles was full of all the sun, warmth, and welcome of a church picnic. But what they failed to mention was that it was actually a desert here. Built on a sunbaked hell that at night plunged down into a cold that would almost freeze at certain times of the year. Like this one.

I looked down the sidewalk and there was car after car, all big and expensive, this being the play area of Los Angeles. To the side was the Hollywood Royal I had just been thrown out of, the hotel of choice for the kids of the stars.

Blood dripped from my smashed nose onto my formerly white shirt, my one good one. This night kept getting better and better.

I reached into my jacket, making sure the sleeve didn't get under the dripping blood, and pulled out my switch. The four-inch blade shot out hard and smooth and I got to work on the tie. My only silk tie because I didn't want to look too out of place tonight in the second-fanciest hotel in Los Angeles. Kind of useless, a tie on me. A ribbon on an ox, but there you have it.

The blade made short work of the tie and I was free. A little clock face in light green silk thread was stitched into the fat end of the thing. I threw that end into the gutter and cut up what was left into two small, thin lengths of just the outside silk. Those I pushed up into each side of my bloody and flowing nose.

Use what you got, it's what my old man taught me. So what if it was silk? Celebrate Christmas with a little class.

Half-a-house no more had steel balls than I did.

He must have loaded up with a steel cup. When you babysit

the wild son of the chairman of National Pictures, you know at some point you're bound to take a shot to the cojones.

Yeah, that's Spanish. I pride myself on knowing foreign languages.

The nose would take exactly fifteen minutes for the blood to stop. It's what it always took.

I looked around for my hat out of habit, then remembered I'd lost it somewhere between the first and second stories on the way down to the pool. It had cost me a sawbuck.

I got up off the concrete slow, my whole body aching and especially the ribs. A pain that felt like a fast hot knife stuck in me.

I should never have taken this case but it was done now. I'd seen what I had been hired to see. The bare ass of Skyler Gold, working like an oil derrick into the fresh earth of a blonde chippie that I didn't need to know the name of. Just the fact that there was one and he was working her, instead of one Abigail Thansom.

Miss Thansom. All of twenty and trying to be grown-up and doing a bad job of it. She was in pain but she would be okay, she just needed a few more bottles of wise-up and she would be fine. As bitter and calloused as the rest of us. Well, the rest of them. I passed callous at sixteen.

Killing a man will do that to you.

I headed up Wilshire to the side street where I had left my car. Ahead, searchlights beamed out from the Hollywood Arms Hotel, cutting into the blackened Christmas sky.

The Hollywood Arms was the older brother to the Hollywood Royal. The younger set went to the Royal, and the real power, went to the Arms.

The Arms was a block of concrete, pushed up out of the ground and set at the back of a front yard the size of five football fields. Palms lined the two entrances and ran along the front of the building itself. The place was almost ten years old but still shone bright like the '20s that were crashing around it.

I liked it, on principal. I did like beautiful things, but something about it struck me wrong. The place was filled tonight, as it usually was, with all of Los Angeles' best, drinking the night away at the Papaya Room there.

Politicians, Hollywood types, gangsters, high-up cops, and low-down attorneys, all of them splashing and toasting, rubbing each other all up and down and setting the world right. Their world.

Mine — ours — out here we could all fend for ourselves.

Or so the thinking went.

Out here a guy had to earn a living, which was getting a hell of a lot harder lately. The stock market had crashed two months ago like a wingless airplane, but while everyone said it was just a temporary thing, I wondered if we were in for a long stretch of hurt. Welcome to the 1930s.

It was almost Christmas and the cold of the LA desert cut through me and all I wanted was a wide, short, clear, solid-heavy glass of whiskey in my hand.

And I would get it at O'Hanlon's Deli, which wasn't really a deli.

Doc would be there, too, as he always was. He could patch me up. That is, if he wasn't already laid out.

That was the problem with Doc: he was always drunk, but he was the best I knew at fixing up anything broken or shot.

Luckily it was only the former, but I didn't hold out much hope that sometime soon it wouldn't be the latter.

Or worse.

www.ingramcontent.com/pod-product-compliance
Lightning Source LLC
Chambersburg PA
CBHW020551180626
46810CB00007B/2458